A DEADLY RIDE

A CHARLETON HOUSE MYSTERY

KATE P ADAMS

ALSO BY KATE P ADAMS

THE CHARLETON HOUSE MYSTERIES

Death by Dark Roast

A Killer Wedding

Sleep Like the Dead

A Deadly Ride

Mulled Wine and Murder

A Tragic Act

A Capital Crime

Tales from Charleton House

Well Dressed to Die

THE JOYCE AND GINGER MYSTERIES

Murder En Suite

Murder in the Wings

Murder Wears Tartan

In memory of Maureen Searle,
a wonderful friend and colleague.

.

A young man wheeled his bicycle past me. He wore a pale khaki army uniform, puttees wrapped around his lower legs, and a rifle slung across his back. The black frame of the bike looked old and tired, the leather saddle as hard as rocks. The soldier doffed his cap as he passed young ladies, winking at those closer to his age.

'Arthur Lumb,' Mark said as we watched him. 'He worked here in the early 1900s. He served in a cycling regiment in the Boer War, then returned to England and worked at Charleton House as a carpenter for the next forty years.'

'Cycling regiment?' I'd never heard of it.

'Great idea, isn't it? Hardly anyone knows about it, but bikes were really useful in wartime and lots of the cycling regiments saw active service on the frontlines.'

'Fascinating, especially with the link to this place. I'd love to know more, if you ever dig anything else up.' Working at Charleton House had rekindled my love of history, and having a friend who soaked up historical facts like a sponge was proving to be useful.

I squinted in the July sunshine and in the distance spotted someone riding along on a penny-farthing. As they got closer, I realised that it was a woman, who looked to be in her sixties, wearing Victorian clothing. She rode easily in a pair of dark-coloured bloomers, her skirt having been gathered up out of the way, smiling and waving at children as they watched open-mouthed.

In honour of the four day Tour of Derbyshire cycling road race, the Duke and Duchess of Ravensbury had decided to throw a celebration of all things cycling. *Charleton House Cyclemania* was being held against the backdrop of their magnificent baroque home, with its grand sandstone exterior and gilded window frames reflecting the sunlight of what had become an extraordinarily hot summer Saturday. As well as an exhibition of antique bicycles, characters from history with connections to two wheels could be seen wandering around the garden and talking to visitors. Glenn Dockett, the silver-medal-winning cyclist from the 1976 Montreal Olympics, was giving a talk and leading some bicycle maintenance workshops. Activities had been planned for children, and old-fashioned competitions like the egg-and-spoon race gave all the youngsters who took part the honour of a plastic gold medal to wear.

Mark disapproved. 'Medals just for taking part? That's the problem with kids these days, sneeze and their mother tells them it's the best sneeze they've ever heard. Teach them they have to work for things, that's what I say.'

'You must make a fun godparent.'

'My godchildren love me. They're the best dressed, that's for sure.'

There was live music, and deckchairs in multi-coloured stripes had been placed around the gardens for visitors to relax on, encouraging them to bring picnics and make a day of it. I had brought in extra café staff, and we had food stalls and ice cream carts dotted around the lawns. If visitors arrived by bicycle, they got their tickets for half price, which accounted for the amount of Lycra on display.

'It's enough to put you off your dinner.'

'Mark, that's a bit harsh.'

'Is it really? An eye full of MAMILs is not going to improve my day.'

'MAMILs?' I asked. He could have been speaking another language.

'Middle-Aged Men in Lycra. Ever since they announced the race, they've been flocking to Derbyshire. No doubt imagining themselves crossing the finish line and being bathed in glory.'

I couldn't disagree. As soon as details about the Tour of Derbyshire had been made public, everyone able to cycle, and a few who couldn't, had dusted the cobwebs off their bikes and had a go at riding the route that had been printed in the local papers. It had become a nightmare for drivers, who'd been spending all their time dodging people who didn't have a clue how to ride safely on the roads.

'What about you two? Surely Bill is keen to get out?'

Mark glowered. 'It's enough to make me divorce him. He came home with a so-called gift for me last night. A pair of Lycra shorts.'

I snorted and had to spit out my coffee before I choked. Mark's physique would make Lycra appear baggy.

'So despite all your carping, you're actually joining the ranks of the MAMILs.'

'Over my dead body. I'm the one who married a retired sportsman, not the other way round. He can go for a ride, and I'll make sure there is witty conversation and an open bottle of wine on his return.'

Bill had actually been a professional rugby player, but it was of no surprise to me that he'd leapt at the excuse to get out on two wheels. Mark's response was equally unsurprising.

'I think there should be some sort of law about who can and

who can't expose the world to the terror of their middle-aged spread under stretched fabric.'

I poked his skinny waist.

'I'd need to feed you a lot more chocolate brownies for that to be a problem for you. So, a bike ride is clearly a no-no. What about we take in the movie later instead?'

On the far side of the garden, a large cinema screen had been set up. In front of it were rows of static bicycles, all ready to be pedalled furiously by visitors, their exertion providing the power for the film projector. The choice of film had been my idea, a fun French animation called *Belleville Rendez-Vous* about a kidnapped Tour de France cyclist who is rescued by his grandmother and dog.

Mark didn't look convinced.

'Hmm, I'm pretty sure it's scheduled to play right around my dinner time, and exercise on a full stomach isn't good for anyone.'

Mother Nature had looked kindly on us. It was a beautifully warm July day and the garden was a riot of colour. With Mark dragging his heels behind me like a distracted child, I wandered over to my favourite flowerbeds, those that were home to the irresistible dahlias and their flamboyant balls of petals. A spiky urchin-like variety with creamy white and lemon yellow flowers caught my eye, standing tall and proud. Another, with rich dark-purple and crimson petals, was a stunning contrast.

The occasional breeze brought with it the heady scent of the rose garden that lay behind a wall. The gardens team had done a fantastic job of creating cycling-themed carpet bedding – according to the little sign stuck in the ground next to one of the beds, the picture of a bicycle had been made using dark-red sempervivums for the tyres and green ones for the spokes. Sedums and more succulents in various shades of green made the frame and a variety of herbs served as the backdrop, while sweet alyssum had been used to create a border around the whole thing. I desperately wished I had green fingers, but knew that realistically I'd spend more time drinking gin in my garden than weeding, let alone trying to be as creative as this.

We walked back towards the house. In the distance I could see visitors enjoying wine at tables scattered between lime and lemon trees on the patio of the Garden Café. Once a baroque orangery, the beautiful light-filled space was now full of chatter and the clink of glasses rather than fruit trees and other exotic plants.

I couldn't help but cast an eye over my staff as they moved between tables. It felt a little like spying, but it didn't stop me.

I felt Mark nudge me. 'Give them a break, I'm sure they're all behaving themselves.'

In the far distance, I spotted the Duke and Duchess. They were holding a picnic for the sponsors who had helped fund today's event. It was unlike any picnic I'd attended, with crystal champagne flutes and solid silver cutlery. A small team of my most trustworthy staff were working as servers under the watchful eye of my chef.

My attention was pulled back by a familiar voice, and not one that I had expected to hear.

'Sophie, Mark, it all seems to be going well.' It was strange to see Detective Sergeant Colette Harnby in casual clothes, her pale-blue shorts and pink t-shirt a sharp contrast to her usual dark trouser suits.

'You actually have a day off?' I asked.

'I do, unless you've stumbled across any more dead bodies recently,' she replied with a smile.

'Not so far,' Mark commented, 'but give her time.'

'Ignore him. I hope you didn't pay to get in? You know one of us will fix you up with a couple of comp tickets.'

'Thanks, but that probably wouldn't be seen as appropriate.'

I decided not to say anything about the countless free coffees and pastries my friend Detective Constable Joe Greene had received off me over the months.

A tanned older man wandered over and stood next to DS Harnby, an ice cream in his hand.

'Meet my dad; he's visiting for the week. Dad, this is Mark Boxer. He works as a tour guide, and is also Watson to Holmes here, better known as Sophie Lockwood, Head of Catering for Charleton House. She runs all the cafés and oversees some of the catering for the Duke and Duchess.'

He gave me a bone-crushing handshake before reaching for Mark, who winced as his fingers were squeezed.

'I believe I've heard about you, Sophie, bit of a knack for finding bodies. So you're responsible for the ice cream as well, I assume. It's delicious and preferable to a corpse.'

I smiled, but changed the conversation. 'What flavour did you choose?'

'Honey.' He licked his fingers as the melting ice cream started to run down the cone. 'Local?'

'Very. We have beehives on the estate and the honey is from those. Glad you like it Mr... Harnby? I don't want to assume.'

'Yes, but call me Paul.'

'Have you heard from Joe, is he enjoying his holiday?' DS Harnby asked. She was Joe's boss, and knew he was part of a motorcycle group that was heading to Italy for ten days.

'Only to say that he had arrived safely, and then something about Stellios? Stellar? Some road he's been dying to ride.'

Paul laughed. 'You mean the Stelvio Pass, every biker's dream, with or without an engine. Forty-eight hair-raising hairpin bends on the north side.'

'Dad used to cycle a lot,' added DS Harnby. 'That's why I thought we should come here today.'

'Well, it was lovely to meet you, Sophie, but I'm guessing you have a lot to do, not least milking some more bees so you don't run out of ice cream.'

Harnby rolled her eyes at her father's 'dad joke', grabbed his arm, and walked him briskly away to explore the day's attractions.

---

2

*A*s I watched Harnby and her father head off across the grass, a fast-moving object hurtled past me. The woman on the penny-farthing was doing another lap of the garden. Behind me, I heard the sound of running footsteps crunching on the gravel path, accompanied by the heavy breathing of someone out of shape.

'I told her and I told her again.' Anthony Leggett, the Charleton House Health and Safety Manager, was sweating in his shirt and tie. He bent forward, resting his hands on his knees, taking great gulps of air before catching enough breath to speak. 'I marked out a route she could take on one of the far paths when there were staff to supervise the visitors and make sure no one walked under her wheels. I told her there were too many people out here on the front. This is the second time I've found her here. I swear she'll be the death of me.'

We watched as he strode off towards the cyclist. She spotted him approach and slowed the bike down. One foot reached backwards and rested just above the little rear wheel, then she smoothly dismounted, giving a little jump as she landed and keeping the bike upright with one hand. Mark and I joined in with the round of applause that she received from the surrounding crowd.

'Olivia Sharp, I need a word,' Anthony called out, while the crowd dispersed and wandered off to find more entertainment or snacks. Anthony wagged his finger as he talked; the object of his wrath, however, appeared to be taking it all in her stride, and I grabbed the opportunity to admire her clothing.

She wore a beautiful short burgundy-red jacket with a high-standing collar and sleeves that puffed up as they reached the shoulder. Her skirt was gathered up at the front, exposing a pair of stout tweed bloomers. They were clearly not the usual underwear that the word brought to mind; these appeared to be designed as outerwear that would be exposed to the elements on a bicycle. It was a curious outfit and I made a mental note to ask her about it.

Anthony and Olivia continued to talk; well, Anthony talked. Olivia smiled stiffly and occasionally nodded, wearing an expression that I read as 'I'll pretend I agree, and as soon as you've gone back to your office, I'll be right back on the bike.'

With Mark occupied by some visitors who had spotted his name badge and were quizzing him on the history of the house, I decided to visit the white tent behind me, home to a display of antique bicycles. Olivia had propped her bike against a metal tent pole by the door and children were gathering, wide eyed, around the penny-farthing, a strange looking contraption that they were unlikely to have seen first-hand before. Its enormous front wheel was almost the same height as me, although I just scraped five feet on a good day.

Olivia had stepped away, mobile phone in hand. It was hardly in keeping with her costume, but then she wasn't Charleton House staff, and so I let it go. A young woman dressed like a suffragette approached, holding a 'Votes for Women' placard and pushing a bicycle. She leant it next to the penny-farthing and walked over to Olivia, and the two women hugged.

I knew the 'suffragette'. Betsy Kemp was one of our live interpreters and she spent her days dressed as characters from history, often those with a link to Charleton House and its owners, the Fitzwilliam-Scott family. Betsy came over to me, nodding towards the penny-farthing

'I reckon you should give it a go, Sophie. I'll give you a leg up.'

'Ha, not a chance. What about you?'

'I already have. Olivia's given me a couple of lessons, but I've not really got the nerve to do much more. Olivia, come and meet my friend.'

The older woman and I shook hands as Betsy explained the link between them.

'Olivia is my father's cousin.'

'She's why I'm here. Betsy was good enough to drop my name into conversation during a meeting months ago.' Olivia's grey hair had been pulled up into a bun, and the high-collared jacket she wore gave her a hard edge, but there was a warmth in her eyes.

'I love your clothing.' Her long A-line skirt was now back in place, the red and purple stripes adding to the vibrancy of her curious outfit. She reached for a cord at her side and pulled. The skirt started to gather at the front, once again revealing her bloomers.

'It's a pulley system, patented in 1895 by Alice Bygrave. There were a lot of women who were rather creative and there are all sorts of marvellous designs out there. They needed to have cycle wear that was practical, but also fitted into the restrictive expectations of society.'

'How clever, and what about the bike? Is it as difficult to ride as it looks?'

'Not really. It takes practice, patience and a bit of nerve, which we all have. You can get on it, if you'd like, although I can't let you ride it.'

I laughed at the mere thought. 'There's not enough coffee in the world would make me brave enough to get on that, but thank you.'

Olivia shrugged. 'Let me know if you change your mind,' she said, turning to talk to an elderly couple who were showing the bike a lot of attention.

Inside the tent were a number of rather old and, in some cases, strange-looking bikes. There were tandems and tricycles; a police bike from the 1920s; a 'sociable' that allowed two people to sit side by side. An immaculate-looking bike from the 1930s had an enormous wicker basket on the front and proudly displayed the name of a butcher's shop on the side. There was a rather tatty black-and-white photo next to it, showing the bike in use by a young lad with a flat cap and an apron tied around his waist.

'That was my uncle, he worked for a butcher in Buxton.' A gentleman in a smart tweed blazer and cap, not unlike that worn by the boy in the photo, picked it up and handed it to me. 'He was given the bike when the butcher's closed down, then when he died, I got it. That's when all this started.' He indicated towards the line of bikes. 'I got the restoration bug and never stopped. Howard Young.'

He offered me his hand. As I went to shake it, I noticed how dirty his fingernails were. His hand felt like sandpaper; I guessed it was the result of years working on bikes.

'Sophie Lockwood, I work here.'

'I know, I saw you helping set up the carts on the lawn. I had a smashing scone from the café inside. The Library?'

'The Library Café, yes. Glad you liked it.'

'I'm partial to a scone, and as it's been a busy morning, I figured I'd earned it.'

I heard a beep; he reached inside his blazer and pulled out a surprisingly up-to-date mobile phone. I suppose it was unfair of me to imagine him using something that belonged in a museum.

'Excuse me, Sophie, something I need to attend to.'

· · ·

By seven o'clock, it still wasn't dark enough to show the film. To be honest, we hadn't thought about that at the project meetings; we'd just got overexcited about the whole concept of a pedal-powered cinema at a cycling-themed event and booked it!

However, the evening was warm and everyone was in a relaxed, lazy summer mood, so no one complained. Groups gathered on picnic blankets, or pulled deckchairs into rough lines in front of the screen. Children in particular seemed to love clambering up onto a static bicycle and pedalling away as though the moment they stopped, the screen would go blank. You could just about make out the film with its ludicrous chase scenes and the quirky antics of its characters. The 1930s music seemed oddly fitting with the backdrop of a stately home that had seen its fair share of lively shindigs in the twenties and thirties.

The smell of a hog roast wafted over the lawns. A local brewer had hand-pulled beers for sale from the back of a van, and for anyone feeling a chill, the most decadent hot chocolate with all the trimmings was an indulgent way to finish the evening.

With the public distracted by the film and no one interested in the displays anymore, Howard Young had started to move his antique bicycles into the back of a van, and I'd watched as Olivia had ridden her penny-farthing out of the gate and towards the car park. She had returned to start dismantling the display boards she had put up and ferrying them back to her own van.

Eventually, Howard sat on the grass to watch the film, a beer in his hand. I recognised the Olympic cyclist Glenn Dockett as he walked out of the house and, along with a young brunette, joined a large group who had commandeered a number of deckchairs. When she'd finished what she was doing, Olivia stopped to watch a little of the film, too.

By 8.30, the film had come to an end and everyone was slowly packing up their belongings. Parents carried tired children, picnic blankets dragging along the grass as they went. The air felt warm and thick as I helped my team return the ice cream carts to the garages we stored them in, then we came back to tidy up.

I helped the gardeners collect rubbish as the pedal cinema team dismantled their equipment, already thinking about the cold gin and tonic that I was going to enjoy in my back garden when the work was done. Charleton House loomed above us, overseeing all our activity with only the occasional glow from a window breaking up its solid black silhouette. Despite being a family home, it looked empty at that moment and, if I'm honest, a little creepy. But the occasional shout between gardeners and the hum of golf carts being driven over the grass, carrying thick electrical cables, added a touch of normality.

I grabbed a big, crunchy piece of crackling from the hog roast stand, and asked the servers to bag me up any that was left over and fill a roll with as much pork as possible. That was my dinner sorted. With all my team dispatched and a warm, greasy paper bag in my hand, it was time for me to head home.

As I set off towards the gate, I heard a shout behind me. It was a man's voice; not a scream, but he needed help. I turned to see one of the pedal cinema operators running towards a gardener, but I couldn't make out what they were saying. The gardener looked around, then waved in my direction.

Why me? What food-related crisis could there possibly be? Then I realised I was the only manager within sight.

'SOPHIE, SOPHIE!'

Smelling like a hog roast, I walked as quickly as I could in their direction. Before I could reach them, they ran further into the garden, and I followed them towards the carpet bedding that had been planted in the image of a bicycle.

The body of Olivia Sharp, the penny-farthing rider, was lying on top of the succulents and herbs. She was still dressed in her Victorian outfit, and the position of her body made her look a little like she was riding the bicycle shape beneath her. I cautiously stepped closer, and the gardener shone his torch on her.

There was something wrapped around her neck, something dark and narrow. A bicycle tyre's inner tube. And it had been used to strangle the poor woman.

*a*fter a fitful night's sleep, I stumbled down the stairs and into the kitchen. I turned the handle of my antique cast-iron coffee grinder; the feel of the beans being crushed between the cogs was deeply satisfying. I took a deep breath, the aroma of coffee beans the only thing keeping me going for the time it took me to make an actual cup of coffee.

Pumpkin head-butted my leg, the force of my solidly built tabby cat taking me by surprise.

'If you won't make my coffee, then you'll have to wait for your breakfast. See,' I demonstrated turning the handle to her, 'it's not that hard. I reckon you could manage it, even without opposable thumbs.'

Sometimes, I think it would be amusing to hear what Pumpkin has to say. At other times, like now, it's probably best that I'm left in the dark, at least until after she has been fed.

Once my espresso had worked its magic, I filled Pumpkin's bowl and listened to her eat, the sound removing any desire I had for food. I was sticking with a liquid start to the day. I yawned so hard I thought my jaw might snap.

I'd spent the night with two images, both of the same woman, swimming around my mind. Olivia Sharp astride her penny-farthing, the children amazed by her, many of the adults in awe of her. Then Olivia lying motionless, an inner tube around her neck, incongruous against the stunning flowerbeds.

In a bid to divert my thoughts from the solemn scene of the previous evening, I turned my mind to the young soldier, played by a live interpreter the day before. Part of me felt I had encountered the real man, or perhaps his ghost – he'd looked so young, so full of life, exactly as Arthur Lumb himself would have done.

Mark's work as a tour guide meant he spent a lot of time carrying out research, so I decided that I would ask him more about Arthur Lumb. Whatever he didn't know already, he'd be able to dig up.

Inevitably, though, it wasn't long before my thoughts returned to Olivia. I could feel my brain cells spark into life as I wondered who could have wanted her dead. She'd certainly seemed like a forthright woman with a touch of rebelliousness about her, but she was into antique bicycles and Victorian costumes, and I could picture her running a local branch of the Women's Institute. Why would anyone have reason to murder her in cold blood?

'Stop it!' I told myself out loud. 'It's none of your business.'

Pumpkin turned to look at me.

'I'm sorry, do you prefer to eat in silence, Your Majesty?' I *was* curious, but this really was none of my business. Plus Joe was on holiday, so I didn't have the ear of my friendly police officer. It was time I kept my nose out and let the professionals do their job.

I knew that the Charleton House gardens would be closed and that DS Harnby and her team would be buzzing around, so I didn't bother to venture up there. Instead, I did the rounds of the cafés and made sure my staff were focused on their work rather than the various fantastic tales that were going around about the possible murderer.

As I returned to my office, I spotted a familiar face.

'Betsy, Betsy, slow down. Are you okay?' I was a little surprised to see her back at work the day after Olivia's death.

'Yes, kind of. I did think about not coming in today, but thought it might be a good distraction.'

'Are you in a rush? Can I get you a coffee, maybe some cake?'

She smiled. 'Thanks, that'd be nice. Then you can start quizzing me about any enemies Olivia had.' I must have looked shocked as she put a hand on my arm. 'It's okay, honestly, it's what I'm hoping you'll do. I'd like to see whoever did this locked up as quickly as possible.'

I decided to take her up to the Stables Café. It was usually busy with visitors when the sun was out, and today was no exception, but up here in the old stables courtyard, Betsy was less likely to be cornered by well-meaning staff, and I removed my name badge to try to avoid being recognised by the journalists who were hanging around.

There was still plenty of Lycra about. A cycle club in matching pink and purple outfits, with calf muscles like large cinnamon buns, had taken over a couple of tables. Children on little bicycles wearing helmets far too large for them bumped over the cobblestones and giggled with delight. I fetched coffee and two red velvet cupcakes, and then Betsy and I settled down at a table on the far side of the courtyard.

'We're not – weren't – that close, to be honest. We shared a love of history, but that's all we talked about, and I only saw her a couple of times a year. When I was younger, she'd send me children's books about women in history. An introduction to the suffragettes, that sort of thing.'

'Was she married?' I asked.

'No, there were some boyfriends in the past, but I never heard her talk about anyone in particular. She still had a full life, though.'

'With the penny-farthing?'

Betsy was picking at the cupcake, rather than taking bites. Mine was half gone already.

'That was a fairly recent thing, the last couple of years, but cycling has always been important to her. She's involved with a couple of cycling activist groups, too.'

It was easy to imagine Olivia standing on the frontline of a protest, demanding we save the planet with the steely voice of a woman not to be messed with.

'She sounds like quite a character.'

'Oh, she was. I enjoyed her company.'

'Do you think she could have annoyed someone?'

'Definitely. She wasn't one to suffer fools. But enough to get killed? I don't know. I don't know what else she was involved with, but I seriously doubt she was caught up in anything dodgy. She was quite a moral woman. In her own way, she was always fighting for what was right.'

Betsy stopped for a moment as two children came screaming past.

'When I saw her to say goodbye yesterday, she was really happy, excited almost.' Betsy was licking frosting off her fingers. 'I asked my dad if he could think of anything, but he saw her as infrequently as me. Said she was strong-willed, but fair. I'm sorry, I've not been much help.'

'You've nothing to be sorry about. It might even be that she accidentally got mixed up in something completely unrelated to her.' I found that hard to believe, bearing in mind how Olivia had been dressed and where she'd been killed, but I couldn't rule it out.

I was determined to stay out of this one, but I was intrigued by Olivia and my heart went out to Betsy. Clearly, I was going to need another piece of cake to give me the strength to fight the urge to get involved.

4

By the end of the day, it hadn't taken my friends much to convince me to finish the weekend in the pub. Mark, his husband Bill Asquith, Joyce Brocklehurst, the Charleton House retail manager, and I drove the two miles in convoy. The Black Swan pub was our 'local', and living over the road from it, I felt like it was an extension of my house. A long row of cheerful hanging baskets on the front of the building gave the already picturesque pub a splash of colour.

We got our usual warm welcome from the landlord, and then, determined to make a start on our drinks as quickly as possible, we went in search of a table in the beer garden. After Joyce had glared for a few moments at a group who were nursing empty glasses, we had a picnic table to ourselves.

Joyce made quite the sight as she lifted first one leg over the bench, then the other, to sit down next to me. It was clearly hard work in a short skirt that was so tight, she had a panty line that would be visible from space.

'Careful, Joyce, you'll pull something,' I warned. 'Do you want to grab a chair and sit at the end of the table?'

'I'm not that old, I'm perfectly capable of getting my leg over,' she replied. I bit my lip so hard I thought it was going to bleed, and Bill's eyes appeared to pop out on stalks, but he didn't say anything.

'You heard it from the horse's mouth,' declared Mark and buried his face in his pint.

'I'm more limber than the rest of you, despite being more… mature,' she commented with a raised eyebrow. Holding on to the hem of her skirt, she slowly contorted herself into a seated position at the table. She was probably right.

'Here's to flexibility and friendship.' Bill raised his glass with a smile on his face and we clinked our glasses. My gin and tonic was perfect. I'd asked the landlord to find something I hadn't tried before which, with a gin list of over seventy distillers, was not hard to do. The gin he'd poured for me had been infused with green tea which, alongside the anise and cardamom, gave it a refreshing, spicy edge.

I closed my eyes and took another mouthful, then another. When I finally opened my eyes again and put the glass on the table, it was half empty and my three friends were staring at me.

Bill glanced down at my glass. 'Steady there, Sophie, I don't want to have to carry you home.'

'Way to go, girl, you've deserved it.' Joyce raised her glass at me and quickly downed half of her prosecco. 'Well, it was fun staring at men's legs all weekend, but I'm glad it's over. Now then, Sophie, what do you need from us?'

'For what?' I asked, genuinely confused.

'To help you work out who strangled Olivia, of course.'

'What I need is another drink and a menu. I'm going to leave this one to the professionals.'

Mark smiled at me with a slight look of disbelief.

'I can help with the menu.' Bill stood and made his way into the pub. I watched his route up the path and my eyes settled on a table near the rose trellis-framed door. A young woman in a smart pale-grey suit was staring intently at a laptop, a slim older man next to her pointing at something on the screen. I recognised him as Glenn Dockett, and she was the dark-haired woman I'd seen him with at the *Belleville Rendez-Vous* film screening. A close-fitting t-shirt emphasised the skinny cyclist's physique that he had managed to maintain. His grey hair was perfectly trimmed; the glasses he removed each time he glanced away from the screen were stylish. He looked like someone who spent a lot of time on his appearance.

'Celebrity spotting?' Bill asked as he placed a menu in front of me.

'Hmmm.' Glenn no longer held my attention now that food was on offer. 'What do you fancy, Joyce?'

I looked at Joyce, but her focus had turned to Glenn. I glanced back at the cyclist and saw that he had also spotted Joyce – not difficult with the sun bouncing off her mound of straw-blonde hair and her rather cheerful choice of a short-sleeved orange satin shirt. The yellow and red blocks that formed her necklace made her resemble a Mondrian painting, a look that was bound to cause heads to turn, especially when combined with alternating yellow and red nails and orange high heels.

The couple's glasses were empty and the young woman put the laptop away, then they stood and appeared to say their goodbyes. I watched as she headed for the car park, and Glenn turned and walked to our table.

'Sorry to interrupt, but you all work at Charleton House, is that right?' We mumbled our agreement.

'They do,' clarified Bill. 'And you're Glenn Dockett, the Olympic cyclist. Pleasure to meet you.'

The two men shook hands.

'I just wanted to say what a fabulous event you all put on. Well, it ended rather sadly, but until that point, it had been a great day.'

I was thinking how nice it was of him to make the effort to come over and tell us this when I clocked that he was directing his comments almost entirely at Joyce. She was responding by gazing up at him, eyes wide open, a slight pout on her lips.

'I'm so pleased you enjoyed it, and I'm so sorry I didn't get to see your talk. I'm a huge fan, but I was just so busy running our rather large retail operation. I'm Joyce.'

It was the first I'd heard about her interest in cycling. She leant across me, catching the end of my nose with her elbow, and offered Glenn her hand.

'I hope you don't mind my interrupting you like this,' he said, 'but I was wondering if you might be interested in going for a drink sometime this week?'

They had clearly entered a parallel universe where only the two of them existed.

'Joyce,' I interrupted, 'why don't you join him now? We were about to leave, weren't we, fellas?'

Mark looked confused. 'But we were about to order...'

'Takeout,' I cut in. 'Takeout pizza at mine.' I emptied my glass and stood up, clambered over the bench and grabbed Mark's arm. 'Joyce, do you want us to save you a slice?'

She waved me off without glancing in my direction.

'No, no, I know what I'm going to be nibbling on tonight.'

She smiled wickedly at Glenn, who grinned back. He had no idea what he had let himself in for.

5

'*O*ne *pain au chocolat*, one breakfast tea and one dead body, please.' Anthony Leggett smiled as he looked down and counted his change.

Anthony was one of the most unpredictable health and safety managers I'd ever worked with. One minute he was berating the Duke for not wearing a hard hat while climbing construction scaffolding, the next he would be putting up a sign in the car park on 1 April, asking people to check under their cars for penguins. On the weekends, he dressed as a Norman knight and took part in historical re-enactments, and each day at work brought a tie with a different cartoon character on it. But still, he worked in health and safety, and I was responsible for a number of kitchens, so I was always on edge when he came anywhere near them.

'Very funny.'

'What? There just seem to be so many round here, I'm beginning to wonder if you can supply them on demand.'

'Well if I can, and do, your paperwork will multiply and you'll find yourself working every weekend, so be careful what you wish for.'

He placed a perfectly neat pile of coins on the desk. I knew without counting that they'd be the right amount.

'I'd come across her before, you know – Olivia Sharp.'

I tried to play it cool as I put the money in the till. 'Really? Small world.'

'Hmm, we had a crisis management exercise, where senior management have to pretend that there's been a major incident and we act out what we'd do. Only round a table, of course; we don't actually start evacuating the building or calling in bomb squads, or whatever it is, but we have someone from each of the emergency services in to answer questions and check all our policies. For the last one, we were asked what we'd do if there was a protest at one of our exhibitions. We had to imagine that one of the sponsors was controversial – an oil company, I think – and that a lot of the visitors in the room turned out to be protesters who suddenly staged a sit in. Our information packs included newspaper clippings about real protests. One was a die-in outside an office block in Manchester, and there was Olivia, pretending to be a corpse in the middle of the road. Sadly ironic now, of course.'

'Have you kept the clipping? I'd be interested to see it.' I could tell from the knowing look on his face that I wasn't fooling him in the slightest. No matter how hard I fought the urge, I had to admit, my sleuthing antennae were beginning to twitch.

'I'm sure that can be arranged.' He gave a little nod and left.

'What was all that about? It's only Monday, you can't have hacked off the Health and Safety department already.' Mark had a look in his eye that I had long since learnt meant he needed a chocolate croissant, immediately.

'We were discussing crisis management. Sit.' He complied and waited quietly for my return, which told me how hungry he was.

. . .

With croissant crumbs all over his moustache, half a mug of coffee downed, and a sugar-based shine returning to his eyes, Mark looked decidedly more human.

'Try these.' I pushed a plate of scones towards him. Over the months, I'd become adept at making a few of the cafés' staple baked goods: cookies and chocolate brownies, mainly. I was the manager of the cafés and not expected to bake, but I enjoyed it, and despite not exactly being a natural, I could now help out with more of the operation.

It was time to master the light and fluffy scones that our visitors loved so much. I wasn't too impressed with how this batch looked – they hadn't risen well, but maybe they'd taste alright and that would be a good start.

Mark grabbed the biggest one on the plate and examined it. He playfully raised an eyebrow and took a bite. Chewing a little more than he ought to with a scone, he took a mouthful of coffee, and then slowly replaced the mug on the table.

'Perfect, Soph, if you want a career supplying hockey pucks. I think I might have lost a tooth.'

I snatched the plate from him. 'Dammit, I thought they might at least taste okay.' I took a bite. He was right; maybe I could pass them off as door wedges.

Mark looked at the plate of half eaten scones. 'Talking of dicing with death, have you heard from Joyce? After we left your place, I realised that we could have just sent her off on a date with the killer. Although nothing could have been worse than the pizza you made us eat. Quite how anyone can burn frozen pizza, I don't know. You work in catering, for heaven's sake.'

'As a manager, not a chef.' I placed another chocolate croissant in front of Mark to make up for the failure of my scones, and he devoured half of it in what seemed like one massive bite. 'I'm working on my baking, but beyond that... well, I'm more interested in eating than cooking. And yes, she's alive. I saw her drive into work.'

'Okay, so if he is the killer, he's not a serial killer. Who else is on your list? And don't repeat any of that rubbish about you not getting involved this time. I know Joe isn't here, but people like talking to you, and you can't help digging around.'

I took a deep breath. He was right and I wasn't fooling anyone but myself.

'I hardly know anything about Olivia, but Betsy can give me a fuller picture of her. Then there are the people at Saturday's event. Like Howard, the old guy with the antique bikes. He can probably give me some background on that world.'

'And Juliet can fill you in on Gorgeous Glenn.'

A hand reached from behind Mark and stole the other half of his croissant.

'Hey, what the...'

Joyce smiled and took a bite of the pastry, returning what was left to his plate.

'Less of the Juliet, I'm more of a Cleopatra. Now, if someone will fetch me something to drink, I will break my usual rule of no kiss and tell.' She spotted one of the café assistants and clicked her fingers.

'Is there any point telling you not to do that?'

'They all know me, they don't take it seriously.' She made herself comfortable in the seat next to me. 'I have a busy day, and I know you want to quiz me on last night, so get to it.'

Mark started to open his mouth.

'Not you, I don't need some inane questions about what time I went to bed, or where I ate breakfast.'

Mark raised his hands in the air and feigned shock.

'Did you have a nice time?' I asked sweetly.

'Lovely, thank you, dear. He's a gentleman, and very good company. He is, however, deeply disorganised, and he knew Olivia.'

'Nice work!' Mark exclaimed. 'Does this mean I've been

usurped and you're now Sophie's partner in crime, her Holmes in heels? Did you pull out the thumbscrews?'

'There's no need for brutality when you have the right skills, Mark.'

'Whatever you want to call them, Joyce, so long as they work.' He glanced at her cleavage, which was getting to enjoy the sun as much as the rest of us.

'Do you want to know what I learnt, or not?'

'Mark, quiet.' I glared at him.

'For a start, he'd forgotten his credit card and I had to pay for dinner. He freely admits that his assistant – you saw her at the pub – organises everything for him, looks after his schedule, even arranges the food delivery to his house. She sounds like a nightmare to me. Bit of a perfectionist, but he clearly likes having everything done for him, which immediately loses him points as far as I'm concerned.

'He does some after-dinner speaking, and I get the impression it's not all for companies with great ethical track records, because Olivia and her protest pals have turned up at some of them. He says he didn't talk to her – he probably left it to his assistant to sort out – and that he didn't see Olivia on the day of Cyclemania. He knew she was there, but didn't run into her.'

'So he didn't hate her enough to go and find her?' I asked. Joyce shook her head.

'No, although I think it's more that he couldn't be bothered. I think his energetic days are far behind him.'

'He can be bothered to chase the ladies,' observed Mark.

'I'm pretty sure he's all mouth and no trousers on that front, too. He's so used to getting everything done for him that I can't imagine many women would put up with him for long.'

'But he was an Olympic champion years ago, how can he afford to pay an assistant and have the kind of lifestyle where everything is done for him?'

'Wise investments. He and another cyclist set up a sports

clothing company not long after he won the Olympic medal. They sold it a couple of years later for an eye-watering profit and he's been living off it ever since. He is also very excited about a new development: he's just signed a contract to be a sports presenter for a satellite channel.'

'Did he show any signs of a short fuse? Do you think he's got it in him to kill someone?'

'Doubt it. He's rather sweet, if you ignore the lazy streak, but I think it translates as "wet". Also, if he'd witnessed anything, we'd have found him cowering in the begonias, convinced that he was next.'

'You did have a productive evening. How'd you get all this out of him?' Mark asked.

'Thumbscrews, darling.' She gave a sly little smile and glanced downwards. 'Thumbscrews.'

6

*H*oward Young lived in a comfortable part of Macclesfield, about fifty minutes' drive from Charleton House. Mature trees lined the street, and every garden was tidy and well kept. I could see Howard as soon as I got out of my car; his garage door was wide open and he was working on an upturned bicycle in the sunlight outside. He stopped what he was doing and wiped his hands on his stained trousers as I walked up the driveway.

'I know you, you make the delicious scones.'

'Well, my pastry chef made them, but I'll happily take credit.'

'Whoever made it, it was one of the best I've ever had. Now then, I find it hard to believe that you're here to see more bikes, although I'll happily show you my collection. Only a few are here, the rest are in a storage unit I rent.'

'You guessed right, and I'm sorry to disturb your day, but I was wondering if I could talk to you about Olivia.'

'Of course. Can I get you a drink first?'

'No, thanks.'

'I'll get you a seat, just hang on a moment.'

He went round the back of the house, giving me a chance to

look around the garage. The walls, floor and every available surface were adorned with bits of bikes; none of them seemed to be whole. Dirty rags, tools, tins of oil – everything you'd expect to find in a mechanic's workshop was there.

A wonderful aroma hovered in the air, a mixture of leather and grease. It didn't smell of dirt, it smelt of hard work, age and my childhood memories, reminding me of my grandfather's shed. He had been part of the generation that fixed things, and had an impressive collection of tools as a matter of course. It was funny how, as I got older, I found it harder to remember names and places, but smells increasingly brought memories flooding back.

A grubby desk in the far corner was home to a laptop with greasy fingerprints on the screen, the once cream mouse smeared with dirt and oil. An online auction site was open.

'I'm bidding on a tricycle, a real beauty by the looks of things. Used to be owned by a family in Matlock who had their own bicycle shop for generations. I like bikes with a local connection. There are a few others after it, but I'm quite certain I'll win. Doesn't run out until tonight so I can ignore it for a while. Come, sit.' Spoken in his deep, sonorous voice, it sounded more like an instruction than an offer.

'Is this a full-time job?' I asked. He laughed.

'Ask my son and he'll tell you it's more than that, it's an obsession. No, I retired years ago; this is just a hobby that's got out of hand. I was a head teacher at a boys' school and an amateur racer. Once I retired, I took more of an interest in the old bikes, and then when my wife died… well, I didn't know what to do with myself. We'd been married for fifty years and I was no longer teaching. I would come out here and tinker with the bikes; I never believed in sitting around doing nothing and I'm not much of a television watcher. After a while, I found that I had been sucked in and it rather took over. But as my wife would have said, it keeps me out of trouble.'

He ran his fingers through his hair, or what was left of it. Without the flat cap he'd worn on Saturday, it was free to stick up in all directions, and he resembled a mad professor.

'Less of my talk, what did you want to know about Olivia? And why is someone who sells scones asking questions?' He leant forward and smiled. 'Not undercover, are you?'

We both laughed, but he quickly looked serious again.

'I know a member of her family and wanted to see if I could help them get a clearer picture of what happened.'

That seemed to satisfy him and he sat back in his chair.

'It's going to seem odd when she's not there – at the next event, I mean. I was getting used to having her around. She could be a bit spiky, but she was a good sort. Honest and direct, that's how I'd describe her. Of course, that can ruffle a few feathers, but don't we all ruffle them here and there?'

'Do you know if she'd ruffled any feathers recently?'

He thought about it for a moment.

'She might have done with her activism, but I don't know much about that. There were probably some youngsters who paid a bit too much attention to her bike and she shooed them off rather ungraciously. You know, I could imagine her giving a piece of her mind to a few youths, and of course, these days you take a risk when you do that. Not like forty years ago when the worst they'd do is scratch your car or shout rude remarks across the road at you. But I've never seen her in an argument with anyone.'

I was looking at the bike he'd been working on. One wheel had been removed and was lying on the ground.

'What do you know about inner tubes?'

'A little. A number of the bikes I've restored didn't use inner tubes; the tyres were solid rubber. I try and track down tubes that are as close as possible to the originals. Some would consider that a bit pedantic as no one would know, but *I'd* know and it matters to me.'

I thought it showed a real commitment.

'Did anyone visit Olivia at Saturday's event? Anyone you recognised? Or did anything unusual happen?'

'Only that girl in the costume – family, I think she said. Other than that, nothing. I'm just sorry I can't be of more help. Olivia was difficult to warm to, but as far as I know, she was a good woman.'

I stood and folded the deckchair he'd given to me.

'Just lean it up by the door, I'll put it away.'

I leant it next to a very modern mountain bike.

'That doesn't look like it needs much work.'

'Hmm, needs a clean, though.'

'You still ride?'

'Heavens, no. That belongs to my grandson. I have two new hips and an increasing sense of my own mortality.'

7

*M*y trip to see Howard had confirmed what I'd expected: that Olivia was part of a world of people passionate about cycling and history. But then, I was surrounded in my day-to-day life by people who loved history, and they weren't killers. I wondered what her activism had to do with all of this, if anything. It was at the very least the reason her path had crossed with Glenn's.

The more I learnt about Olivia, the more I liked her. She seemed like a strong, determined woman who'd lived a full life with purpose. She was the kind of person I liked the idea of becoming in my old age, rather than the madwoman at the end of the road with twenty cats who has a gin and tonic for breakfast, which was the more likely outcome at present.

I drove through the Charleton estate, past grazing sheep and deer. Some had taken shelter from the sun under trees and decided to stay there. After all, food was immediately on hand – they just had to drop their chins. There were still a few walkers out. I passed a couple walking on the road, their legs – unused to seeing the light of day – appearing burnt and sore. The house had just closed and a line of cars was nosing its way out of the car park. Some visitors lingered, ice creams in small, sticky hands. No one was in a great hurry – another warm summer evening lay ahead.

I pulled into a parking bay and spotted a couple of familiar faces: Bill had arrived to collect Mark from work. I'd already been told that Bill had a surprise for him, but looking at the expression on Mark's face, it wasn't the kind of surprise he wanted. Then I saw the two bikes strapped to the roof of the car. No wonder Mark wasn't over the moon.

'Hello, chaps, off to recreate the Tour of Derbyshire?'

Bill laughed. 'Maybe a mile or two of it. I borrowed these off a colleague at work who has a habit of buying a new bike each year. We're having such beautiful evenings, we ought to make the most of them. I thought it would be fun to explore more of the estate on two wheels. We'll park over at the farm shop, and then noodle around some of the lanes and gravel tracks nearby. It'll be nice and quiet.'

Mark turned to face me and, with his back to Bill, mouthed, 'Help me.' Bill appeared to be checking the straps that secured the bikes, and once he was happy, he patted the roof of the car.

'All set. Ready, Mark?'

'Of course, darling,' Mark replied, continuing to look at me with bug eyes.

'Have fun.' I gave Mark the biggest smile I could muster. 'Next time, I expect to see you in Lycra. It would really suit you.' I was sure that if I'd got close up, Mark's pupils would have been replaced with little daggers.

'Sophie, Sophie.' Anthony Leggett was making his way out of the security gate, digging around in his briefcase as he walked. 'I have that newspaper clipping for you.'

He didn't look up as he searched for it, nor did he stop walking, so it was no surprise when he slipped off the kerb and stumbled. Showing no sign of having noticed, he kept walking in – roughly – my direction.

'Here it is.' He brandished the piece of paper above his head, then handed it to me. It was a photocopy of an article from the *Manchester Evening News*. 'Hope it helps. Goodnight.'

'Thanks, Anthony.' I watched him lollop off; he had a way of moving that made it look as if his joints weren't quite connected properly. I just hoped he checked for penguins under his car before he drove off.

Later that evening, relaxing in my back garden, the newspaper article on my lap, I ran my fingers through my lavender plants. Eight pots of the things were lined up along the edge of the path as I hadn't got round to planting them. If I was honest, we'd probably reach autumn without my getting round to it.

The scent of lavender was something I found immediately relaxing. I often went in search of it within the Charleton House gardens if I was having a particularly stressful day. It wasn't often I spent time in my own garden, and as I sat down on a scruffy wooden chair that I couldn't remember ever having used before, I regretted not doing it more often. My small garden looked out across the rolling hills of Derbyshire, and a patch of trees in the distance was the only thing preventing me having a view of Charleton House, although I could just see the top of the folly that stood part way up the hill behind it. I was convinced that I had once seen the sun glint off the pineapple-shaped weather vane that was its highest point, but I could have equally had something stuck to my glasses.

I watched as Pumpkin stalked a stick in amongst the weeds that dominated the flower-free beds and reminded myself of the need to get some advice from the gardeners. I wanted my garden to look pretty with as little work as possible. Make that no work at all. I was aspirational, but ultimately lazy in the garden department. Maybe plastic grass was the way to go.

Pumpkin eventually gave up the chase and sprawled on the

warm concrete slabs next to me, occasionally rolling and stretching and collecting bits of gravel and twigs in her fur. I lazily scratched a finger behind her ear and sipped my gin and tonic; I'd filled it to the brim with ice, which not only kept it cold longer, it also limited the amount of tonic I could fit in.

I looked more closely at the newspaper article on my lap. The photo it showed was of an office block in Manchester and the street outside. Dozens of cyclists and their bikes were lying in the street, looking for all intents and purposes like the victims of a mass hit and run. On the pavement was a large group, many in cycling shorts and helmets, holding banners, although they were out of focus and I couldn't read what they said.

In the middle of the photo, one of the 'dead' cyclists was immediately recognisable as Olivia, which backed up what I'd already learnt about her: that she was one to take action when she felt strongly about something. The year-old article told how the MD of the region's biggest minicab firm, Thorne Cars, had made a comment at a shareholders' meeting that an increase in the number of deaths of cyclists was inevitable as the number of cyclists rose, and was largely down to the cyclists themselves being untrained. The cycling community was, unsurprisingly, in uproar.

I vaguely recalled the incident from last year; it had made the local TV news channel. Stephanie Thornton, the managing director, had initially remained unrepentant and stood by her comments. But after a few weeks, she had attempted to backtrack, claiming she had been quoted out of context and ploughing money into cycling projects. The article quoted Olivia and described her as the organiser of the protest. I could see why Howard might think her activism had made her enemies.

I felt a sudden stabbing pain in the end of a finger and looked down. Pumpkin was staring up at me, the hook of one claw sticking into my fingertip. It appeared that family time was over and she'd had enough attention for one evening.

Very slowly, I unhooked myself and she ran off to the end of the garden. I folded up the article and placed it on the table. Protesting against minicab firms didn't seem particularly contentious to me, at least not when compared to siding with political revolutionaries or calling for the release of prisoners, which was how she could have spent her retirement. I struggled to see how campaigning for cycle safety could lead to murder.

I let my thoughts drift and took my time enjoying my drink. As the sun set, a slight chill crept in; just enough for me to need a sweater or a blanket over my knees, so I decided to call it quits and head inside.

I was getting ready for bed when my mobile phone beeped. Bill had sent me a photograph. As it opened up, I burst out laughing, and the accompanying story made me laugh even harder. I was still giggling to myself as I drifted off to sleep. I couldn't wait to see Mark in the morning.

8

I'd had another restless night as Pumpkin woke me multiple times by walking across my pillow, each time standing on my hair and nearly pulling it out at the roots in the process. Come the morning, I crawled into work in desperate need of more coffee, the single espresso I'd had at home barely enough to get me from the front door to my office. This was a bad sign for a Tuesday – far too early in the week to be struggling already.

I kept my own bag of my favourite coffee beans in my desk drawer and just the smell of them formed a smile on my lips. My staff beavered away, tossing the occasional sympathetic glance my way, and left me to stare at the water as it slowly sank through the coffee. Making any kind of coffee was the closest I came to performing a religious ceremony, and anyone who knew me well knew not to disturb the process.

I burnt my tongue as I took the first sip, but with the next few mouthfuls, I could feel myself standing straighter. My eyes opened a little more and the words that came from my staff started to make sense to me.

I grabbed some paper from my office and took a seat at a table out in the café; I wanted to consider the information I had gathered about Olivia so far – what little there was of it. Every inch of wall space in the Library Café was covered by books, hence its name, and I tried to suck inspiration out of them by osmosis, but I was still staring at a blank piece of paper ten minutes later when the doors crashed open, swung closed again and bounced back open.

A voice shouted from the other side, 'CAN SOMEONE HOLD THE DAMN DOORS OPEN?'

A café assistant dashed across the room and awkwardly held the doors apart. Mark, slowly and with a complete lack of grace, navigated his way through the doors on crutches, his leg covered in a plaster cast. I wondered if he'd let me sign my name on it, just like we'd done at school whenever a child turned up with an arm or leg in plaster.

I pulled a chair out and helped him sit, laying his crutches on the floor by the wall. A coffee appeared before him and I mouthed 'Chocolate croissant' at the young man who had brought it over.

Despite his injuries, I was impressed that the rest of Mark was as manicured as ever. His moustache was perfectly twirled and he had on a tweed waistcoat with a bright turquoise lining and a matching pocket-handkerchief. The waistcoat was one of my favourites, and every time he wore it, I threatened to steal it.

'How are you feeling?'

'Cumbersome, and I've been given a desk in a storeroom next to the cleaner's cupboard. All I can smell is disinfectant, it's making me dizzy.'

'You'll be able to get back up the stairs to your normal office when you're used to the crutches, though?'

'I imagine so, but they're a nightmare, and I want to make sure I don't overdo it.'

And prolong the sympathy as much as possible, I thought, patting the back of his hand.

'Of course, dear.'

'Don't patronise me, I was involved in a serious collision.'

'Why didn't you tell Bill you couldn't ride a bike?'

'It never came up. Besides which, when you're trying to impress an ex-professional sportsman, telling him you can't ride a bike is unlikely to get you his phone number.'

'It's very sweet you're still trying to impress him.'

'Oh heavens, not now, those days are long gone. I meant when we first met. Now he knows what a splendid deal he bagged himself.'

'Clearly not.' I grinned. 'Anything else you've not told him?'

He put what was left of the croissant in his mouth, successfully dodging the question. Once he'd swallowed, he changed the subject.

'So, how goes the investigation? I'm sure it's going to slow down without me to assist.'

'To a snail's pace. Well, so far I know that Olivia was strong-willed, passionate, and inclined to hack people off with her protests.'

'Any suspects that stand out?'

'None. At this point, I'd normally bribe Joe with a coffee and a croissant and see how much information I could get out of him, but not this time. Glenn is the only person I know with any kind of link to her; other than that, I'm rather flying blind.'

I needed some fresh air. I often found that I thought better when I went for a walk.

'I'm heading to the gardens, you coming?'

Mark glanced down at his leg, and then gave me a look of incredulity. 'Seriously?'

'Of course, come on. I'll grab you a wheelchair from the visitors' office. The fresh air will do you some good.'

. . .

Mark was seated in an old wheelchair. It was the only one the Visitor Services department had available to loan me, a busload of octogenarians having arrived first thing. The wobbly and unsteady chair clearly hadn't been used for a long time and was only one step up from a shopping trolley with a wonky wheel.

I pushed Mark along the lane to the side of Charleton House and paused so that security could raise the barrier. I was about set off again when a golf cart came to a screeching halt beside us. We stared, more than a little surprised at who the driver was: Joyce.

'Mark, what have you done? Annoyed one little old lady too many? Forgotten to look before crossing the road? Importantly, are you alright?'

'Fine, thank you, Joyce.'

'Excellent. Then I don't feel bad about calling you a bloody idiot. Off to the gardens?'

I nodded.

'Hang on, you don't know if it was my fault,' cried Mark.

'Was it?'

'Well, there was a tree… and I hadn't been on a…'

'You're an idiot. Get in.' She tapped her sunflower yellow nails on the steering wheel. 'Come on, I've not got all day.' I helped a nervous-looking Mark out of the wheelchair and into a seat, leaving his chair with a concerned security officer. My bottom was barely on the seat when Joyce slammed her foot onto the pedal and the cart shot forward. We flew under the barrier, out through the car park, narrowly missing a head-to-head collision with a visitor's car, and were heading for the entrance to the formal gardens. We bounced over cobbles, hurtled over potholes, flew over speed bumps, and weaved around squirrels.

'Bloody hell, Joyce, what's on fire?' I shouted. She responded with what can only be described as a cackle.

'Always wanted a go on one of these,' she called over the wind that the speed was creating. 'Never been able to think of an excuse before, but I need to go and oversee... OUT OF THE WAY—' she bellowed at an elderly couple who had stepped onto the path '—the dismantling of the gift stall in the garden now the police have given us access.'

Mark was gripping onto a metal bar, his knuckles white. We were heading for a small gap in a stone wall where staff would check tickets. Joyce beeped her horn and the staff leapt to safety just in time.

Joyce resembled a modern day Boudicca at the head of her chariot. Only Boudicca had worn less leopard print and didn't have large yellow plastic hoops swinging from her ears. We were now on a tightly packed gravel path, the wheels kicking up dust and leaving a trail of weaving tyre tracks. I saw my life flash before my eyes as we took a corner at full speed. Mark was clinging on to my arm so tightly, I was convinced he was going to draw blood.

'Slow down!' I shouted as we headed for a tight bend. I hadn't expected to need life insurance when I took on the role of Head of Catering, but then I hadn't expected to participate in an extreme sport either.

'To hell with that,' Joyce called. 'Hold on.'

Mark was thrown against me and I held on with all my strength, desperately trying to avoid being hurled out of the cart. I could have sworn we'd taken the corner on two wheels. Visitors, wide-eyed with horror, were left staring after us. Joyce swerved around a gardener, drove onto the manicured lawn in order to avoid mowing down a small child who was focusing on his ice cream, bounced back onto the gravel, and then slammed on the brakes.

We skidded to a halt. Mark and I sat in dazed silence.

'I'm going to see how the gang are getting on and collect some boxes, see you here in fifteen?' Joyce didn't wait for an answer and disappeared into a white tent.

I looked at Mark. 'You okay here?' Mark looked back at me.

Well actually, he sort of looked through me. I wasn't sure he knew where he was anymore.

I slowly levered myself off the seat and clambered out, leaving Mark alone to contemplate his near-death experience. Then I walked, or rather weaved on jelly legs, towards the flowerbed where Olivia's body had been found.

9

I spotted Robin Scrimshaw, the head gardener, kneeling by the large, colourful flowerbed that Olivia's body had been found in. He was replacing plants and recreating the image of the bicycle that had been crushed by her body and the police.

'Hey there, Soph, stretchin' your legs? It's another glorious day. Shame about all this.' He sat back on his heels and looked across the bed, shaking his head. 'Poor woman. Wonder what she did to deserve this, but I reckon you're goin' to tell us.' He smiled warmly. 'Just kiddin'. But I guess a few people are puttin' a bit of pressure on you.'

'Not really, just a few jokes here and there. But you know me, I can't help myself.'

'Well, fire away, I'm sure you've a few questions for me. Although I wasn't here when it happened, I was puttin' away power cables. I came back over when the police arrived cos I figured they'd have questions for someone who knows the layout of the grounds well, and I needed to round up my team. Some of 'em were getting a bit too inquisitive. Human nature.'

'I'm rather surprised there weren't any witnesses. There were a couple of hundred people in the garden at least.'

Robin stood up slowly, his hands on his knees forcing him up. He stretched out his back.

'Aye, but they were all looking in the direction of the screen. We didn't need any lighting out here even when it did get dark, and if you think about it, the cinema guys' van was just here, blocking the view. We're lucky she was found before morning. I'm glad, though. That it was dark, I mean. The only other time I saw a body, I had nightmares for weeks.'

It was Robin who had found the body when someone was killed at the Charleton House Food Festival the previous year. I was relieved he hadn't been the first on the scene with this one too.

'Dreadful way to go, 'specially for someone who loved bikes. By the way, do you need any inner tubes? I don't mean to be morbid, but we've got loads, and tyre-changing kits and a bunch of other stuff. They were in those goody bags that people were given at the bike maintenance classes. That cyclist chap was handing them out. They had latex gloves, a little Allen key set, some of those sports energy bar things, an energy drink – all sorts. Whenever you give away gift bags like that, a lot get left behind. People don't want to carry them home or forget them. My lads collected a load of them when they were tidying up.'

Great, so any Tom, Dick or Harry could have got their hands on an inner tube and be a potential murder suspect.

'No thanks, I don't have a bike.'

'No worries. Well, if I hear anything that I reckon will help your investigation, I'll give you a shout.'

He lowered himself back to his knees and focused on the plants. I'd watched him work many times before, but this time seemed different. He was a little slower in his movements, seeming to take greater care, show even more respect for where he was working than he usually did. He was a sweet man, and the right man to be working on this particular flowerbed.

Mark was deep in conversation with Betsy – who was dressed as an Edwardian lady – as I walked back towards him, and Joyce was ferrying boxes from the tent and piling them in the back of the cart. I felt distinctly disheartened after discovering how easily to hand the murder weapon had been, but I plastered a smile on my face for the sake of the others.

'Call yourself a gentleman?' I shouted over at Mark. 'Why aren't you helping Joyce?'

He looked up at Betsy, a pathetic expression on his face.

'Do you see what I have to put up with? No sympathy. She'll have me washing dishes in the kitchen by the end of the day, just you see.'

Betsy grinned at me. 'He sounds fine.' Mark gave an exaggerated pout at her comment. 'I saw you all arrive, at some speed,' she added with a raised eyebrow, 'and wanted a word. The police have said we can have access to Olivia's house tomorrow and I need to go and turn off the water, empty the fridge, that sort of thing. I thought you might like to come with me. You might find something useful, and to be honest, I could do with the company.'

'We'd love to join you,' Joyce chimed in as she arrived with another box. 'We'll bring a bottle of wine and toast her.'

I could see Betsy visibly relax. 'Thank you so much. I didn't really fancy going on my own, not yet. That's a lovely idea, Joyce. Olivia was partial to a glass of chardonnay, she'd appreciate it.'

Joyce turned up her nose. 'Chardonnay? If we're going to toast the old girl, it will be with a bottle of fizz and no less. We'll do it properly.'

In the distance, a man wearing a light three-piece suit and a straw boater hat was waving frantically at Betsy.

'I better go. I'll text you the address.' She opened her parasol and started off across the grass.

'What about me?' asked Mark. 'My leg's in plaster, not my lips, I can still drink.'

Joyce put her hands on her hips. 'I'm afraid, my dear, you've been usurped. There's a new Watson in town.'

'What's that about Watson?' None of us had seen DS Harnby approach across the lawn. 'I hope Sherlock hasn't been pulled into service.' She eyed me suspiciously. 'Yes, I know what your friends call you.'

I was about to respond when Mark did it for me.

'We'd never dream of sticking our noses in, would we?'

Joyce and I shook our heads and muttered a few words of support.

'Glad to hear it. I know how things work with you and Joe, but while he's getting his knee down in Italy...' She glanced at Mark, who had a look of confused surprise on his face. 'I said knee *down* – it's motorcycling terminology, not an innuendo.'

I laughed out loud. Harnby hadn't known him long, but she'd quickly got the measure of Mark.

'While he's away,' Harnby continued, 'we'll be playing this strictly by the rules. I ask the questions, you all get on with your day jobs. To the best of your ability, at any rate.' She was eyeing up Mark's plaster. 'What happened to you?'

'Skydiving.'

She smirked.

'Hey, I could skydive if I wanted to.'

DS Harnby shook her head as she walked off to join her boss, Detective Inspector Flynn, and the Duke who were waiting for her. She was probably going to have to explain to DI Flynn what was so funny and why she hadn't appeared to be giving us a strongly worded warning about minding our own business. One thing was for sure: her calm, polite warning wasn't going to have its desired effect. I couldn't wait to get to Olivia's and see what else I could find out about her.

10

Keeping a house like Charleton going is an expensive business, and an important part of funding it is finding and holding on to sponsors for special events. We had a new exhibition of paintings due to open in the autumn, and today the Duke and Duchess were hosting a lunch for those companies and individuals who had already agreed to provide support.

The artist, Derbyshire born and the latest 'hot property', would be giving a talk and hoping to charm a little more cash out of those in attendance. It was to be a relaxed, intimate buffet lunch for twelve people in the Duke and Duchess's light-filled private dining room, a space that was never open to the public. You had to be family, a private friend, royalty, or very rich to find yourself welcomed into this room. In reality the Duke and Duchess rarely used it, except for birthdays and Christmases, so it wasn't as much of a glimpse into their private lives as it might have seemed.

My head chef was in charge of producing a light summer menu. As he prepared the display of miniature wild mushroom tarts and the salad made entirely of ingredients taken from the

Charleton House kitchen garden, his assistant was laying out fish platters and a selection of cold meats that were being served with pickles, one of which I knew the Duchess had made herself. The Duchess had also prepared the table displays, deciding on delicate light shades. Pale pink roses, cream hydrangeas, Queen Anne's lace and grasses were part of her chosen decoration, larkspurs giving a pretty pop of blue.

Servers in crisp white shirts polished glasses and I folded napkins, looking for all the world like the work-experience teenager no one trusted with anything breakable. To be honest, my assistance wasn't really needed, but I never missed an opportunity to spend time in parts of the house that were normally off limits to me. The cream and gold wallpaper reflected the light that streamed in through the large windows, the landscape paintings on each wall creating the illusion of further windows looking out onto the estate as it had been in centuries past.

I was admiring the detail on a tulipiere in the white marble fireplace when I heard the Duchess's voice. She had the first of the guests with her, and I could hear others close behind, so I stepped out of the room and pulled the door only partly closed, watching from the shadows of a narrow corridor as they entered the room. It was fun to see people's reactions as they encountered the magnificence of the house for the first time. Some took in the space with a sense of awe and wonder that I could relate to; others played it cool, attempting to give the impression that this sort of thing was old hat to them. Pastel-coloured summer dresses and linen suits, no ties, were the dress code of the day.

One woman caught my eye as she arrived. Her elegant powder-blue trouser suit was simple and beautifully cut; her long, dark hair hung loosely down her back. She looked cool and relaxed. I watched as she took a glass of sparkling wine from a server, gazed around the room, and then, with a strong and confident voice, called to the Duchess. She seemed to feel very at home.

She was also oddly familiar to me.

I checked my watch. It was time to stop feigning usefulness and avoiding the work I really needed to get on with, so I made my escape down plain narrow staircases and corridors like the servant that I would have been in years gone by.

I wanted a cold drink, and so decided to show my face at the Stables Café. On the sunny side of the back lane, it was warm, but the sun was blindingly bright and I squinted, cursing the stinginess that had resulted in my refusal to pay for prescription sunglasses. Living in England, I wasn't convinced I'd get enough use out of them, and then long, hot summers like this made me regret my decision.

Using my notepad as a sun shield, I passed through the security barrier, waving at the security officers with my free hand, and nearly slammed into the back of a young woman who was standing in the middle of the path, tapping furiously on her mobile phone. I did that terribly British thing of apologising, despite not being the one in the wrong.

'Hmmm? Okay.' She hadn't even noticed that I'd nearly sent her flying. I recognised her as soon as she looked up from her phone.

'You work for Glenn Dockett, right?'

'I do, and you are? Oh, you were at the pub the other night with…'

'Joyce.'

She smiled and offered me her hand. 'Amber Tate, I keep Glenn on the straight and narrow.'

I laughed. 'What's he doing at the house?'

She looked confused. 'Glenn? He's not here. Ohhhh, you think I'm with him. No, I'm here to collect Stephanie. She has a luncheon with the Duchess.'

'Stephanie?'

'Stephanie Thornton, she runs Thorne Cars. The company is one of the sponsors of an art exhibition.'

Something clicked in my mind. *That's why the woman in the powder-blue suit was familiar.*

'Was she at Cyclemania on Saturday, at the picnic?' I asked, trying to hide the excitement in my voice. Amber nodded.

'She was.'

Two big jigsaw pieces slotted together. A woman who had good reason to want Olivia out of the way had been here at Charleton House the day she'd died.

I needed to spend some time with Amber.

'Are you in a rush, or do you have time for a coffee?'

She looked momentarily surprised at the suggestion.

'Sure. I was about to find a café to work in while I wait for Stephanie. Where do you suggest?'

'Follow me. I know a couple of places round here!'

I found us a table outside the Stables Café and fetched a couple of iced coffees. The stone walls of the courtyard did a good job of keeping the sun out of our eyes and the cobbles underfoot seemed to suck in some of the heat. It was a lovely, cool spot.

'Does Glenn take a lot of managing?' I was asking more for Joyce than myself. He hadn't scored full marks the other night, but he might be keen to convince her of his suitability for the role of 'Mr Right' and I was going to look out for her.

'All the time. He's a really nice guy and I enjoy working for him, but I doubt he'd find his way out of the house in the morning without me. He'd attend every event with a set of spanners sticking out of his back pocket if I didn't keep an eye on him.' She reached into her bag and pulled out a screwdriver to illustrate the point. 'How many women do you know who carry this sort of thing around? I had to take this off him last night before he presented an award at the Manchester Velodrome.'

'So what does your job involve, other than checking his pockets?'

'A bit of everything. I suppose you could say I'm responsible for the image of Glenn that the public gets to see. I find events for him to talk at, I make contact with journalists, get him sponsorship deals, and recently I've managed to get him a couple of TV jobs. His racing days are long over, but he's great in front of a camera. Later this year he'll be commentating on all the international cycling events for a small satellite channel. This has all come rather late in his life, but he's very well respected and has a few more years left in him. But only a few, so we have to get this right. Until now, most of his work has been with magazines and overseas TV.'

'It looks like all your hard work is paying off.'

'I hope so.' She sipped her cold brew and looked around.

'Do you do the same thing for Stephanie?'

Amber shook her head. 'She doesn't need that kind of minding. She's very organised. I'm much more a traditional PR for her, a consultant. I'm not on her full-time staff.'

'I guess the two jobs overlap. Thorne Cars seems to have a lot to do with cycling.'

'Yes, I've been working with Glenn for a while. Most of my career has been associated with cycling. I was doing a bit of part-time work for Stephanie when she… well, hit a bump in the road, and I could help the company work on its relationship with the cycling community.'

I knew exactly what she was referring to, and it wasn't exactly a bump in the road, unless you included the bodies of those who'd participated in the die-in outside Stephanie's offices. I was surprised at how open Amber was being with me, but then it had been all over the papers, so there really wasn't a lot of point in trying to hide anything.

'Glenn's profile was starting to rise and he was a good choice to help front some of the projects and events we set up.'

'Did Stephanie face much of a backlash?' I asked.

'Initially yes, there was a lot of publicity. But it's like anything

– a few days later, the press moved on to something else. Stephanie still has her critics, but they aren't gaining the same kind of attention.'

'Critics like Olivia?' Amber looked confused for a moment. 'The woman who was killed.'

'Oh, her.' I felt the atmosphere shift. It hadn't become cold, not quite, but a barrier went up. 'That was very sad.'

'But you know who she was?'

'Yes.'

It was clear she wasn't going to say any more than that without me pressing, which told me a great deal.

'Did you see her on the weekend?'

'Only in passing. Why?' Amber sounded genuinely curious.

'I'm just trying to get a picture of the day that Olivia died. It's hard with so many people around and it was starting to get dark by the time everyone was leaving.'

Amber drained her plastic cup, which made a rattling sound as she got more air than liquid. She looked a little embarrassed and quickly put the cup on the table.

'Why are you so interested?'

'Olivia was related to a friend of mine. I just want to help her put this behind her as quickly as possible, and knowing what happened removes confusion and uncertainty.' Olivia's relationship with Betsy had become a convenient excuse for my interest; it was better than saying *I'm a nosy parker with a growing reputation for getting involved in police business.*'

Amber shook her head. 'I'll be honest, we were never that pleased to see her. Glenn was always very polite, but that was it. The cycling world can be quite small, but the collectors, the ones into the vintage bikes, are a different part of it. We mostly mix with athletes or attend events with a modern cycling theme, so there's no reason for our paths to cross. I don't think I'd have recognised her if she wasn't astride a penny-farthing.'

I had more questions for her; I wanted to know how much

contact Stephanie had had with Olivia, but we were disturbed by her phone ringing, and as she started to talk, I could tell it was going to be a long call. She mouthed 'Sorry' and 'Thank you' as she pointed to the cup. I smiled and left her to it.

So Amber was tied to someone who had reason to be frustrated with Olivia. I wondered just how far her loyalty would go to protect their reputation. With that thought rattling around my head, I walked into the Stables Café to hover over my staff, getting under their feet. If I didn't do that at least once a day, I could hardly call myself a manager.

11

J'd reluctantly agreed to Joyce driving us to Olivia's. After the experience of her behind the wheel of the golf cart, I did wonder if it was the wisest choice I'd ever made. She owned a bright blue BMW convertible, the top was down and her headscarf blew in the wind like Isadora Duncan's. Only with a better outcome, I hoped.

I was pleasantly surprised by the smooth journey as we followed the curve of the country lanes with Marvin Gaye singing in the background.

'Any excuse to get the top down and I'll take it,' she called out. I was glad Mark wasn't there to comment. 'She's a beauty, isn't she?' Joyce patted the steering wheel. 'The only good thing to come out of marriage number three.' She glanced over at me. 'On the subject of marriage, when are you and Joe going to stop tiptoeing round the issue and actually go on a date? A proper date, mind, not just coffee when he drops by the house.'

'You get straight to the point.'

'Life's too short for anything else. So?'

I stared out across the fields, trying to put together my

answer. I'd missed Joe while he was away, but not as much as I thought I would.

'I really like him, but he's sort of like a brother.'

I paused and thought about how sweet he was, all the glances we'd shared across tables, and how pleased I was every time he walked into one of the cafés or when he joined us at the pub for a drink.

'Go on.'

'I guess I like the idea of something more with him. He ticks all the boxes for the ideal boyfriend, but I just can't get excited about the idea. Besides which, I'm really enjoying being single. I like my own company, quiet nights in after a day dealing with demanding customers and even more demanding staff. I don't feel like there's anything missing from my life.'

Joyce reached over and gave my hand a squeeze.

'That's because there isn't anything missing from your life. But you should talk to him. I think he's tiptoeing round the subject because he's shy about broaching it, not because he's unsure of what he wants. Let him move on.'

'You're pretty good at this. You should have your own agony aunt column.'

She let go of my hand. 'I'm great at dishing out advice, but not following it. My problem is I believe in Mr Right and I am on a quest to find him. And while I'm doing that, I'm too busy having a lot of fun with the various Mr Right Nows that cross my path to heed my own advice, so I leave a trail of broken hearts behind me.'

'Is that what Glenn is, a Mr Right Now?'

She winked and grinned as she turned up the music and started singing along with Marvin.

We pulled up outside a red-brick semi-detached house on the kind of smart-looking street I imagined to be inhabited by teachers and solicitors. The driveway was empty, but I had no idea how Betsy was travelling here, so it didn't mean she hadn't arrived.

Overgrown bamboo formed a canopy across the path to the house and we had to crouch a little as we went. Betsy opened the door before I had a chance to ring the bell.

'Hello, ladies, come in, come in.' She peered beyond us. 'Where have you parked? I left the driveway free for you.'

'On the side of the road,' replied Joyce, 'just in case you hadn't arrived yet and wanted to park on the drive.'

'Ah, never mind.' Betsy looked as if she'd been crying. 'I'm in the study, collecting a few things for my dad. I half expected to find it in a bit of a state, but the police seem to have been really respectful.'

The carpets were plush and soft underfoot and I regretted not taking my shoes off, but it seemed a bit late now.

'Lavender?' I asked as we walked into a large room at the front of the house. Betsy smiled.

'Yes, she loved the stuff. There are little bags that she sewed herself all over the place, and the garden's full of it.'

It was just another reason for me to like Olivia. I was really starting to wish our paths had crossed much earlier and I'd had the chance to get to know her.

One wall of the study was filled with dark wooden shelves. A roll-top desk stood against the chimney breast, and two old-fashioned wooden filing cabinets stood against another wall. I loved that style of cabinet, but I'd yet to find one where the drawer didn't stick. The room was refreshingly clear of electronic clutter.

Betsy was going through a cabinet drawer as she talked. 'Dad told me where she kept things like her funeral plan and I said I'd dig them out.'

Joyce was looking at the collection of black-and-white photographs on the wall and I took a seat at the desk.

'Please, help yourself,' Betsy said over her shoulder. 'I know the police have already been in here, but you might find something they missed.'

My interest was drawn by neat piles of paper, a beautiful speckled-red fountain pen in a carved walnut stand and a bottle of ink. Betsy noticed me handle the pen.

'She insisted on handwriting notes. You'd never get a thank you in an email, she didn't think that was personal enough.'

I flicked through the papers. Bills, newsletters from a historical cycling organisation that clearly hadn't taken the electronic route either. Nothing really caught my eye.

I joined Joyce looking at the photos on the wall. There was a group of suffragettes on bicycles, one of a woman on her own wearing almost the exact same outfit that Olivia had worn at the Cyclemania event. A vintage poster had a woman pedalling away and the line 'Chains that set women free' underneath it. A well-worn suffragette's sash had been framed and hung above the desk.

'You said her interest in the penny-farthing was fairly recent?' I asked Betsy, who had moved on to the bookshelves.

'Last couple of years, yes. Not just penny-farthings, she wanted to build a small collection of bikes. I think it was the perfect mix of history, women's rights, and what she thought of as beautiful objects. They all come together with the bicycle. I suggested she start looking at the clothing, too. I knew she could sew and I thought she'd enjoy the research.'

'Who's this?' Joyce had taken a seat and was waving a black-and-white photo of a woman on a bicycle at us. Betsy took the photo from her and smiled.

'That's Florence Ida Adamson. She was one of the first female magistrates in the country, in 1919. Come with me, I want to show you something.'

I was familiar with the role of a magistrate; I had an aunt who had been one for thirty years. They were lay people, also called justices of the peace or JPs, who heard court cases in their local areas, dealing with less serious criminal cases. When I was a child, I would call my aunt a jacket potato, having no real understanding of what she did.

We followed Betsy into the kitchen and through a door that led into the garage. The penny-farthing I'd seen Olivia ride was hanging on a wall. The contents of a large cardboard box lay strewn on the floor, and a vintage bicycle was leaning against a workbench. Betsy ran her hand over the saddle.

'This was the delivery the neighbours took in yesterday. Olivia had only just bought it; she won an auction on the weekend and told me about it when we caught up at Charleton House. This bike used to belong to Florence, the woman in that photo. The family didn't want it anymore and stuck it on an auction site. Olivia was so excited. Florence went everywhere on it – there are photos of her attending rallies, and she even rode it around France, alone. She sounded like quite a force to be reckoned with.'

'Not unlike Olivia,' I added with a smile.

'Ha, yes. Olivia wanted to recreate the outfit in that photo and take the bike to events. It needs a bit of a clean-up, but it's a great find.' Betsy fell silent.

'Perhaps you can do it,' I suggested, 'in her honour.'

She immediately brightened. 'You know, that's not a bad idea.'

We tidied up the cardboard and went back into the house.

'Wine?' Betsy asked.

'That's a splendid idea,' replied Joyce happily, proceeding to pull a rather expensive looking bottle of champagne out of a cooler she'd brought with her. 'I reckon Olivia deserves the decent stuff.'

12

We sat on the patio in the warm evening sun, overlooking the slightly overgrown garden. One end was nothing but a mass of lavender, and of course I'd been unable to resist running my fingers through the flowers before I sat down.

Joyce poured us all a glass and Betsy led us in a toast to 'A woman with more energy, determination and passion than most people put together.'

I sat back and allowed the sun to heat my eyelids. Joyce was savouring her champagne and letting out a satisfied little sigh after each mouthful. Betsy was turning the pages of an old photo album she had retrieved from the bookcase. I could see small black-and-white pictures of young men and women with bicycles on what appeared to be camping trips, picnics and group shots outside cafés.

Betsy noticed my gaze. 'Olivia grew up on a bicycle and was forever organising outings for her friends.'

'Did she have a tendency to take charge?' I asked, wondering if she could be bossy, domineering, maybe condescending into the bargain, enough to really annoy people.

'I'm sure she insisted on having the final say in a few things. She wasn't perfect. She and my dad had some real humdingers, but she never held grudges. He said she was always the first to make contact again after a row.'

'The more I hear, the more I like,' said Joyce, flicking through the photo album. 'She was quite the looker in her youth – she's surrounded by the lads in these photos.'

'But hard to get,' laughed Betsy. 'When I was a teenager, she was always telling me to focus on my studies instead of the boys in class, and that had always been her approach, too. I don't think she ever minded not being married. She led such a full life.'

'Hey, Sophie…' Joyce was holding the album up towards me when the sound of squeaking metal and wood being dragged across the ground caught my attention. I looked at Betsy.

'What's that?'

'No idea, but it's coming from the front of the house.' She turned her head and listened as the sound was repeated. 'That's the garage door.'

With Betsy in the lead and Joyce bringing up the rear, we all got up and, resembling a slightly rag-tag version of Charlie's Angels, crept around the house along the side of the garage, pushing undergrowth out of the way as we went, until Betsy raised a hand for us to stop.

Two narrow slit windows ran along the top of the garage wall. I climbed unsteadily onto a pile of broken breezeblocks and peered in. The garage doors were wide open and a white van was parked on the driveway, its own doors also open and facing the garage.

I stepped down to find Joyce removing one of her shoes and wielding it like a weapon. The stiletto heel did look rather threatening.

'What good will that do?' I whispered.

'Depends where you aim it,' she replied with a wicked tone to her voice, pulling a face and pretending to stab the air.

'Shhhhh,' Betsy warned us. She peered round the corner of the garage for a moment, and then turned back to us. We could hear banging in the back of the van, and then footsteps in the garage. 'I'm sure there's only one person. When I say, we run out, shut the van doors and keep them shut.' She looked round the corner again and I heard the sound of someone clambering back into the van. 'Ready... Now.'

We sprinted, or in Joyce's case hobbled, to the back of the van. Following Betsy's lead, we slammed the rear doors shut and threw ourselves against them. From inside came an almighty crash and a lot of shouting. It was a male voice. The door started to shake, but he didn't stand a chance with the three of us leaning up against it.

Betsy pulled her phone out of her pocket and dialled.

'Police,' she said, a little out of breath.

'Pipe down!' shouted Joyce towards the occupant of the van. 'Or I'll think of somewhere to stick my stiletto.' It was only then that I noticed the champagne glass in her other hand. I doubted that she'd spilt a drop.

By the time the police arrived, Joyce had put her shoe back on and emptied her glass. We'd passed the last ten minutes perched like a row of birds on the rear bumper of the van, making sure the doors remained shut, and Joyce spent most of that time complaining about the dent that was being carved permanently into her bum. She was somewhat appeased when the two police officers who arrived turned out to be reasonably good looking.

We told them what had happened and stepped away from the van door. They swung the doors open, and we were faced with the rather sorry sight of Howard Young sitting on the floor, Olivia's recently purchased bicycle next to him.

'I could arrest you for false imprisonment,' DS Harnby said as she joined her colleagues. Her voice had lost its friendly tone.

'But we stopped him getting away,' I whined, quickly realising that whining wasn't going to get me taken seriously.

'And you could have noted down the registration of the vehicle. We'd have got him eventually.'

'Well, we sped up the process for you.' Joyce raised her glass at DS Harnby and I noticed that at some point she'd managed to top it up. Harnby looked back at me.

'I hope you're driving.'

'I am now,' I reassured her.

'I'll have one of the officers take your statements, and then you can go. I mean it. Please, leave.'

With wide eyes and a tight mouth, Harnby glared at me, but as she turned away, I saw a smile creep onto her face.

13

*B*efore I'd even opened the door of the Library Café to the visitors, Mark was sitting at what was becoming his main desk. It was now Thursday and he'd had plenty of time to practise slowly hobbling up the flight of stairs to his office, but I enjoyed having him around, and he knew to scarper when the café got full and customers needed his table.

He was hard at work when I carried a couple of scones and two mugs of coffee over.

'What are you doing?' I asked.

'Completing my edible masterpiece.'

It dawned on me what he was up to. Over the weekend, the catering team had made simple round shortbread cookies and sold them with little tubes of pre-made icing. Children could then decorate their own biscuits. Many had turned them into bicycle wheels with spokes, others had decorated them as medals. Now, Mark was creating a rather pretty pattern with multi-coloured dots that were spinning out from the centre of the biscuit.

'Is this your pointillism phase?' I asked.

'Well done.' He sounded surprised.

'I'm not a complete philistine, I know one or two things about art.'

'I put you down more as a Vettriano poster kind of a girl.'

'Snob. Drink your coffee.'

He took a sip and then placed his mug back on the table. 'So, fill me in. Now that I've been cast aside as no longer fit for purpose, I'm going to have to hear about your adventures after the fact.'

I told him about Howard and allowed him to picture Joyce with a stiletto brandished above her head.

'I miss all the fun. Well, I'm trying to remain useful, so I went home last night and spent my time online.' He slid a pile of papers towards me. Flicking through them as he took a bite out of a scone, I kept half an eye on him, waiting to see his reaction. He started off chewing happily enough before slowing down.

'Okay?'

'They're a bit... I don't know. They taste funny.' He took another bite, and from the look on his face, I knew the exact moment he realised what he was tasting. 'Salt. This thing's full of salt.'

I picked up the other scone and tried it, realising immediately what I'd done.

'Dammit, the ingredients are all in similar jars. I didn't read the labels properly. I'm an idiot.'

I pushed the plate aside. He waved the papers at me.

'When you're done trying to poison me, do you fancy taking a proper look at these?'

'What am I looking at?'

'Olivia's tree-hugging activism has been playing on my mind. Plenty of opportunities to annoy people there, so I thought I'd find out more about the protests she'd been involved with. There are a few road-building protests – she was even involved in one against the closure of cycling paths in Derbyshire where the protesters stripped to their underwear to highlight the "stripping away" of safety measures. There are no photos of that one, fortunately.

'This one interested me, though: it was against building on the greenbelt just outside Manchester. There are a couple of familiar faces there.' He spun the printout of the grainy black-and-white photo towards me.

I stared at the photo, casting my eyes over each face one by one. Mark nodded when I pointed at Olivia. I kept looking.

'I know her!' I exclaimed. 'That's Stephanie Thornton.' She was one of four people in suits in the background. They were watching over the protesters with folded arms and scowls on their faces.

'I did a bit of digging. She's an investor in the company that was trying to build the houses.'

'Trying?'

'The project got shelved after the protestors took their fight to the courts and won a delay. That was eighteen months ago and the project remains on hold.'

I grabbed Mark's hand. 'I could kiss you.'

'Oh, go on, I'd love to hear the gossip after being seen locking lips with you.'

I had been thinking more of a peck, but he was right, it would be very funny.

'Hello, love birds.' Joyce strode into the café. There seemed to be an extra bounce in her step, and her hair – I could have sworn her pile of blonde locks was getting gradually higher and higher. I let go of Mark's hand and waved at one of the café assistants, mouthed *'Coffee'* and pointed at Joyce. The young girl smiled, looked in the direction of my pointing finger, and then scuttled off to the barista station with fear in her eyes. Joyce had a way of snapping at my staff that I hadn't yet managed to put an end to.

She reached for a scone and, before either of us could warn her off, took a bite. It was a matter of seconds before the expression on her face turned to one of disgust.

'Holy hell, Sophie, what is this?'

'A failed attempt at...'

'It's failed alright.' She washed it down with a mouthful of Mark's coffee. 'You missed out on all the fun last night, Mr Boxer.'

'Sounds like it, and how is Mistress de Medici this morning?'

'Who?' asked Joyce, with a wary scowl.

'Catherine de Medici, first woman to wear high heels. Only she used them to increase her height, not threaten men with. She was queen consort of France from 1547, so she's a similar age to you.'

'I'll break your other bloody leg for that.'

'Coffee.' The young assistant appeared at just the right time, placed the coffee before Joyce and darted back to the counter. Joyce turned to face me.

'I have something for you.' She pulled a couple of photographs out of her bag. It was turning into a morning of show and tell. 'I was about to point these out to you when we were disturbed last night. They were in the photo album Betsy was looking at.'

One was a black-and-white photo of four young people lying on the side of a hill, their bicycles scattered around them. They were laughing in the sunshine. The second photo just had one of the couples, staring into one another's eyes, a cigarette, or more likely a joint, lazily hanging from the young man's fingers. Based on the age of the photo and the people's clothing, it appeared to have been taken in the early 1970s.

'Does Betsy know you've got these?' I asked.

'No idea, but she won't mind. Go on, look.'

I looked more closely. A young Olivia was laughing, leaning back against the young man, his arms around her, and it looked as if he was tickling her. The picture might well have been taken over forty years ago, but the man was immediately recognisable: it was Glenn Dockett.

. . .

'Hello, Glenn, it's Joyce.'

Mark and I sat in silence as Joyce made the phone call.

'I'm well. I was wondering, I have some free time this afternoon – how do you fancy coming to the house and meeting up for an hour or two?' She sat back in her chair as she listened, uncrossing and re-crossing her legs. Quite a sight in a skirt short enough to qualify as not much more than a belt. 'The Garden Café? I'll leave your name at the main gate and you won't need a ticket. Why don't we meet there at three? … Yes, me too… it was lovely…' She hung up. 'He's smitten.'

'Smitten enough to tell us the truth?' I asked uncertainly. Joyce stared at me intently.

'In this skirt, I reckon he'll tell me anything we want to know, and if that fails, I've always got the heels.'

'And what do you mean by "us", Soph?' Mark added. 'Joyce never said anything about having you tagging along on her date.'

'Didn't I?' Joyce feigned an angelic look. 'It must have slipped my mind, but I'm sure he won't mind being interrogated by two lovely ladies. It was good timing. He's coming straight here from a private school just outside Macclesfield – he's giving a motivational speech to the older students and running a bicycle maintenance class for the younger ones.'

'Wish we'd had speakers like that at my school,' grumbled Mark.

'I'm guessing you didn't go to some fancy-pants fee-paying school with an endowment fund that makes my mortgage look like small change,' replied Joyce.

'You're right there.'

'Well, don't worry, love.' She patted his hand. 'They did a reasonable job of turning you into a semi-functioning member of the community.'

He shoved a piece of scone into his mouth and scowled at her before glancing at me and swallowing with an uncomfortable-looking gulp.

'Now, now, children, I'm sure we all have work to do,' I declared, standing and clearing the mugs and plates that were scattered around the table. Joyce waved one hand in the air.

'I'm on a go-slow day, so I'll stay here and keep Mark company for a while. I'll have another coffee, Sophie, if you don't mind.'

Mark slumped his shoulders in mock disappointment. As I made the coffee and split a croissant between them, I looked over. They were deep in conversation over something Mark was showing Joyce on his phone. For all their teasing and barbed comments, they shared a fondness for each other that gave me the warm and fuzzies on the rare days I got a glimpse of it.

I was looking forward to our meeting with Glenn; it was starting to feel like we were learning a few things that could be useful. But our investigation was made so much harder by Joe's absence. Even if he couldn't tell me exactly what the police had learnt, which he sometimes did, he could at least give me some indication of whether or not I was heading in the right direction. I didn't have any of that without him.

I looked up from another batch of scone dough and saw DS Harnby through the window. She spotted me and waved. Scraping off as much of the dough from my fingers as possible, I ran outside.

'How did it go?'

'How did what go?' she replied suspiciously. I could tell she knew exactly what I was getting at.

'Howard Young. Was he just after the bike, or does he deserve a closer look?'

'No comment!'

'Oh, come on. Just tell me this: is he still at the station, or is he currently enjoying a cup of tea in his own home after a rather unfortunate lapse in judgment?'

She sighed. 'A well-respected retired head teacher is suffering greatly after the loss of his wife. His grief has led to some mistakes which he deeply regrets, and which will be followed up in the appropriate manner. He is currently at home and may well be drinking a cup of tea. He might also be enjoying a digestive, for all I know.'

She looked at my hands. 'Are you baking, or grouting tiles? Either way, why don't you get back to your job and I'll get back to mine?'

I held the sides of my skirt and pretended to curtsey before running back inside. So, I knew that Howard Young had been arrested for attempted theft only, so far. It wasn't much, but it was something.

I looked down at my skirt. Big floury handprints were firmly planted on each side where I'd held it when I'd curtsied. It was a wonder I was ever taken seriously.

14

*J*oyce and I had taken a table in the corner of the Garden Café. The crisp white tablecloths, the sparkling silver cutlery, the light streaming in through ceiling-high windows, and the single cream rose in a slim cut-glass vase on each table all worked to create a rather dream-like atmosphere. It was one of the three cafés I managed, but the one I felt least comfortable in. I was much more a country pub and roaring fire kind of girl.

Joyce had swapped over her earrings as we sat down, and was now touching up her lipstick. Glenn might well be just Mr Right Now, but she was still making an effort. I spotted the disappointment on Glenn's face as soon as he walked in, but he had the good grace to make it sound as if I was the highlight of his day.

'Sophie, this is a bonus I wasn't expecting. You're looking well.' His dark hair was only slightly grey around the temples. The wrinkles had set in, but gave him a healthy craggy look. His pale-blue shirt was tieless and his navy suit looked crumpled in a stylish linen kind of way.

'You're incredibly clean for someone taking a bike mechanics class,' I said with surprise. I'd been expecting to see oil on his clothes.

'It's called hands-on learning, or let the little buggers do it themselves.' He grinned and hid his hands under the table. 'Just don't look at my nails.'

We chatted about his work at schools and how things had settled down here at the house since the weekend, but there was an air of expectation that was starting to gnaw away at me. I felt as if he knew we had an ulterior motive, so I gave Joyce a nudge with my elbow.

She took the hint. 'Glenn, we wanted to talk to you about something.' She popped open the clasp on her handbag and brought out the photograph of the young Glenn and Olivia. Her scarlet-red fingernails stood out against the faded image and were a little more bloodlike than I was comfortable with, but that could just have been my overactive imagination. Glenn pulled out a pair of glasses and perched them on the end of his nose, glancing up at us as he did so.

'No escaping the ageing process, I'm afraid. Not that either of you needs to worry about that for a long time yet.' He was, in some ways, a classic charmer, but he managed to pull it off without seeming creepy.

He looked at the photo and went quiet. His rugged features seemed to drop a little, and I could have sworn that in the time he took to register who the photo was of, he had aged even further.

'Aaah. Where did you get this?' he asked with a hint of frostiness. Joyce ignored it.

'Olivia was your girlfriend?'

He sat back and looked at his hands. Glancing at both of us, he sighed.

'A long time ago. We met in a cycling club, had a couple of summers of fun, and then my professional career took off and it just became too difficult. I don't think she was too upset; I don't think she was ever the marrying kind.'

'Do the police know about you and her?' I queried. He gave a fantastic demonstration of squirming in his seat, but said nothing. 'Why on earth not?' I demanded.

'How would it help?' he exclaimed. 'I wasn't involved and I have no idea who killed her.'

Joyce put the photo away and took over the questioning. 'Didn't your paths cross at all? Not even a hello? You must have seen her at Cyclemania on the weekend?' She was rather good at this. I'd half imagined her interrogating him while either holding him up against a wall or sitting on his lap. Instead, she was calm and collected, innocently curious.

'We'd said hello from time to time, but that was it. Nothing that could help with an investigation.'

That just confirmed what Amber had told me on Tuesday. 'So why not say that?' I asked. 'It's harmless enough.'

'It's taken me years, but I've finally started to get some TV deals, and at my age that's incredibly rare. I should by rights be pottering off to the scrap heap. The last thing we need now is the press sniffing around and putting my name next to that of a murder victim.'

'We?' Joyce looked confused.

'Amber, my assistant.'

'How much does she know about your history with Olivia?' I asked.

'Most of it. She's done a great job of putting a positive spin on all my exes and less than successful business ventures, but she would like me to settle down. She says a steady girlfriend, or better still a wife I can keep hold of, would help the image.' He looked at Joyce, a smile hovering at the corners of his lips. She ignored it.

'Does Amber fancy you?'

He laughed at her question. 'God, no. She's like my daughter, I think I permanently exasperate her.'

I didn't sense an ounce of attraction on his part, nor on hers when we'd chatted on Tuesday. That didn't feel to me like a lead worth following.

'When did you last talk to Olivia?' I asked.

He thought about it for a moment. 'About six months ago. I was invited to give a speech for a company's annual dinner. The organisation was on her radar for being involved with the destruction of some woodland or other. Whatever it was, she didn't think I should be associated with them.'

'Did you give the speech?' I queried. He sighed.

'I have to pay the bills somehow.'

'What about Stephanie? You've done some work for her, right?'

'I have, corporate gigs. What about her?'

'I know Olivia didn't make life easy for her company. Do you know if they met face to face, or did Stephanie have her staff do all that?' I'd given up pretending that this was anything other than an interview.

'Oh no, she's had words with Olivia a couple of times. Thorne Cars is a pretty big company, but Stephanie is still very hands on. Her dad started it with a single car over thirty years ago and now it's a mini empire. She's very protective.'

'How protective? How serious were these "words"?'

'Well, Stephanie does have quite a temper on her. I've seen her fire people on the spot. But I never worried about Olivia, she can more than hold her own.'

We all descended into silence. It didn't take long for it to start to feel uncomfortable, so I got up. Glenn did the same.

'Thanks, Glenn.'

'No problem. Joyce, lovely to see you again.'

She smiled warmly.

'I'm going to an event on Saturday night,' he added. 'Not a big thing. It's another sponsorship event, Thorne Cars are having their staff summer party. Would you like to join me?' I knew he was asking Joyce, but I think I squeaked at the mention of

Stephanie's company. It would be a great opportunity to sniff out more information.

'Sure.' She glanced at me. 'But I come as part of a pair.'

Glenn did a great job of hiding his disappointment again.

'Sophie? That's a great idea. I'd love to have you both along.' It seemed he was a great actor as well as a great cyclist.

15

J'd returned from the Garden Café to a note from Mark.

Come to my office. Bring cake (not scones).

With a bag of white chocolate cookies and a scone just to freak him out, I set off across one of the courtyards and in through the door marked 'ladies toilets'. Before entering the main room with the cubicles, I took a quick right turn up a flight of stairs marked 'staff only'. This route, which confused and concerned many first-time visitors seeking Mark, took me to his office. The windows were wide open and a fan in the corner of the room was creating a gentle ripple of paper across all the desks.

'You decided to give the stairs a go?' I asked, impressed.

'The café got busy and I figured it was time. Betsy here gave me a hand.'

Dressed as a Victorian house servant in black skirt and shirt, white apron and cap, she looked uncomfortably hot.

'I hope the visitors appreciate you in all that get up.'

Betsy fanned herself with a magazine and puffed. 'Nope, all

they want to know is "Have you ever worked at Downton Abbey?", cheeky sods.'

I offered her a cookie. The lumps of white chocolate had melted, which as far as I was concerned was when they were at their best. I gave Mark the bag with the scone in it.

'So why did you drag me up here?'

'Pull up a chair, ladies.' He propelled himself across the room on his office chair to a meeting table. Betsy and I joined him in less dramatic style.

Mark took a photograph out of a folder and handed it to Betsy. It was a black-and-white image of a woman in early 20th-century clothing, standing next to a bicycle.

'Recognise her?'

'That's Florence Ida Adamson, the magistrate whose bike Olivia bought.' Betsy passed the photo on to me. The bike appeared to be in slightly better condition, but as far as I could tell it looked the same as the one in Olivia's house. I was impressed that Mark had been paying that much attention when I'd filled him in on the finer details of our visit to Olivia's house the previous night. I'd expected the image of Joyce stalking a hapless burglar, stiletto heel held aloft, would have wiped all else from his memory banks.

'Now, take a look at this.' He handed me another photo. The face was different, but the clothing was familiar. The young man was dressed in military uniform, and it was that which told me who it was.

'I'm guessing it's Arthur Lumb,' I said. Mark nodded.

'You showed some interest in this chap the other day, so I thought I'd find out a bit more. I think you're both going to like this. Look at the bikes.'

Betsy and I leaned in and examined the photos more closely. We put them side by side.

'Is that the same bike?' Betsy asked, her voice full of disbelief.

'I think so, yes. Arthur had been raised in London and that's where his immediate family was. When he came to Derbyshire after the war, he stayed with his aunt and uncle and two cousins. The elder was a girl called Florence. She was quite sparky for a girl of her time and was one of the young women who discovered the freedoms a bicycle could bring.'

'Our Florence?' Betsy asked with surprise.

'The very same. She was a campaigner for women's rights, an advocate for equal pay and better pensions for women. She helped raise money for a maternity and child welfare centre – I would guess she took an interest in that as a younger sibling died during childbirth. After the Sex Disqualification Removal Act of 1919, she became one of the first female magistrates in the country.'

He stopped, but neither of us knew what to say in response.

'I reckon that if we look closely at the bike your aunt bought, we'll see where the gun carrier was attached,' Mark continued. 'The holes for the screws will still be there. It's just too much of a coincidence. I guess Arthur gave the bike to his cousin if he was no longer using it – he probably had some sort of sentimental attachment to it having brought it all the way back from Africa, but this was keeping it in the family. I have more research to do. I think Florence might even have had a connection to Charleton House, but I've not got that far yet. I have a pile of old records still to go through.'

'That's incredible.' Betsy was wide eyed. 'It shows what a small world it is.'

'Back then, this sort of thing was quite common. Everyone knew everyone else, and almost everyone would have known someone who worked up here at the house at one time or another. It was a major local employer.

'Betsy, I got some help with my research from the museum in Buxton. When I told them what I was doing, they asked if there was any way your family would consider loaning them the bicycle? They would love to do a small exhibition on both Arthur and Florence.'

'Of course. I mean, I'd have to check, but I can't foresee a problem. I reckon the family would love that.' Betsy was beaming.

'Mark, thank you.' I squeezed his arm. 'This really is amazing.'

Betsy had a photograph in each hand and looked transfixed. 'She sounds incredible. What women like her achieved was mind-blowing. There's not many like her around now.'

Mark looked across at me. 'Oh, I wouldn't say that. I've met a couple of impressive women while I've been here at Charleton House.'

was beginning to wonder if there had been a shift in tectonic plates and England had nudged closer to the Costa del Sol, but even my vague memories of schoolgirl geography told me that the plates weren't laid out like that. Still, the seemingly endless hot weather did make me feel like I was on holiday. I'd be taking a siesta, learning to flamenco and indulging in tapas next.

We had the food covered at any rate. The Black Swan did a fantastic selection of bar snacks and our table was covered in a drool-inducing array. A charcuterie board was going to be my first stop, padrón peppers with flaked sea salt were next on the list, then it was an all-out fight between the mussels served with leeks, cider and mustard crème fraiche, and a couple of Scotch eggs that I knew would be cooked to crispy perfection on the outside, and inside, the egg yolk would be beautifully soft. Of course, that all came with two bowls of chunky chips and plenty of ketchup and mayonnaise to dip them in.

Mark grabbed a chip and inhaled it. Bill, who had just arrived with a tray of drinks, shook his head.

'I do apologise, I'm sending him to a ladies' deportment school as soon his leg is healed.'

In response, Mark repeated the performance, and then sucked his fingers clean with agonising sound effects.

'Ignore him,' said Bill, 'and with any luck he'll go and sit at another table.'

'So, do we get an update?' Mark asked as he passed me the large glass of gin and tonic. I raised a finger in the air, requesting one minute to savour the juniper notes of my drink.

'Aaah. Yes you do, soon.'

Two padrón peppers later and I was ready to tell all. Now that Howard was off the list, I moved on to Glenn and his links with Olivia.

'Do you really think he could kill an old girlfriend?' Bill asked, not looking so sure. I explained my thinking to them.

'When emotions are running high and someone has a lot to lose, then I guess anything is possible. Also, in one of the photos he seems to be smoking marijuana. It's no big deal in the grand scheme of things, but you know how much of a hot topic drugs are in pro cycling these days. If Olivia had evidence that he had a track record with any kind of drugs, then it could have got him a lot of adverse publicity. Even if she had no intention of sharing that information, it might have scared him. And now he's close to some level of success that he's been after for years, and at his age it will absolutely be his last chance, maybe he could be driven to kill someone.'

'And if he doesn't have anything to fall back on...' Mark offered, looking at his husband, a retired professional sportsman who was now a teacher.

'True. I knew that I couldn't play pro rugby forever so I made sure I planned for what would come after. I loved the sport, but I didn't have any desire for it to be my sole focus for the rest of my life, so when the need to transition into another career came, I was ready. There are plenty of others out there who have made their sport the centre of their lives. When it comes to an end, they're lost. Some genuinely don't want to do anything other than stay in that world forever, and I'm guessing that Glenn is one of those. So, do we need to worry about Joyce?'

'Why would we ever need to worry about Joyce?' mumbled Mark through another chip. 'Apart from being as scary as hell, she's pretty sharp. I don't think she'd stick with a man who she has the slightest doubt about. A lot of her past is still somewhat mysterious, but I'm guessing she's been through enough and got enough scars that she won't needlessly waste her time.'

'True, but still, there's no harm in keeping an eye on her. I'll have a word, make sure they meet in a public place and she's never on her own with him. And I'll tell her to text me regularly.'

I agreed wholeheartedly with Mark's assessment of her character. I'd pity anyone foolhardy enough to take Joyce on, but still, I'd never forgive myself if anything happened to her.

'I'm still wondering about the protests,' I said. 'There's plenty of opportunity for Olivia to have made enemies there. But when I talk to anyone, they say she was strongminded but respected, and I would guess her associates in the various groups she belonged to would say the same. One thing I don't understand, though, Mark: why were the Duke and Duchess happy to have Thorne Cars on board as a sponsor after Stephanie Thornton's comments and the resulting protest being in the press? I'm surprised they wanted to continue working with them.'

Mark shrugged. 'It wasn't that big a deal. The phrase *"today's news is tomorrow's chip wrapper"* is pretty apt. Besides which, Stephanie worked really hard to rehabilitate the company's reputation. When she got her driving ban, she worked doubly hard. The company ploughed money into cycling schemes, paid for cycling safety lessons in schools, sponsored sports events – they are even minor sponsors of the Tour of Derbyshire. She'd turned a small taxi firm run by her dad into a major regional business, and I think the Duke has a soft spot for people who pull themselves up by their bootstraps. She'd done her time, so to speak, handled it all really professionally, and she's now a great supporter of the house. I met her once when she was on a tour I was leading. She's a lot of fun.'

'Did you say driving ban?' I hadn't heard anything about that before.

'Yes. She must be about halfway through it by now. She'd had one too many at a dinner and drove her own car home. Ridiculous really, she has a whole fleet of drivers. But she took it on the chin. The papers covered it for a couple of days, but she didn't try to hide anything from them so it wasn't quite as scandalous as they would have liked, and they moved on to their next big story pretty quickly.'

'Wow! She has a driving ban? I don't pay any attention to the news these days. I wonder if there's anything else, public or not, that it would be useful to know? I'll have a chance to find out more on Saturday. Joyce and I are going to an event Stephanie is running for her staff. Glenn will also be there, so I'm hoping I can chat to him after he's had a couple of drinks. Maybe he'll let a few things slip. Maybe I'll find out more about Stephanie at the same time.'

'Just be careful.' Bill wagged a finger at me.

We spent the next hour devouring the food, ordering more and not leaving a crumb. Finally, Bill looked at his watch.

'We need to go, I still have some marking to do. I can hardly have a go at the kids for handing in their work late if I do the same thing. Come on, Peg Leg.'

'I'll clear all this,' I offered, 'you head home.'

'Oh, before we go, I have something for you. Dessert.' Mark reached into his rucksack and handed me the paper bag containing the scone I'd taken to him when we met with Betsy. 'You can't fool me that easily.'

I laughed and watched the couple make their way slowly up the gravel path and out onto the street. They were deep in conversation and missed the familiar face that was looking for an empty table. DI Mike Flynn had a pint in one hand and a packet of crisps in another. I hoped for Joe's sake this wasn't about to become Flynn's local, otherwise his relaxing visits to the pub might quickly become a little less relaxing.

I stacked the tray high with dirty dishes and glasses. It seemed my table clearing work was never done.

I left the tray at the end of the bar and waved my thanks to the bar staff, turning round just in time to see DS Harnby walk in. Joe really was going to have to find somewhere new to relax with a pint if both his boss and his boss's boss were drinking in here now. Then I saw Harnby's dad walk in and remembered he was visiting.

Harnby spotted me and I waved. She sent her dad off to the bar and walked over.

'I'm surprised you've time for a drink,' I said with a smile. I wanted her to know that it wasn't a dig.

She nodded towards her dad. 'Playing tour guide when you've a murder investigation on isn't ideal, but the least I can do is buy him dinner. Now I've seen you, I must ask: is what I'm hearing right? That Joyce is dating Glenn Dockett?'

'I wouldn't call it dating, but they have spent some time together. Why? Is he a "person of interest"?'

'Don't read too much into my question, I'm just curious.'

'And I'm curious about your curiosity.'

'Just tell her to be careful,' Harnby warned.

'Is she at risk? Come on, you can't tell me that and leave it there.'

'No, I don't think she's at risk. She's proven she's more than capable of taking care of herself, but we are looking at him.'

I knew this was never going to be as clear-cut as someone being annoyed at an ex, but Harnby had just given me the impression I was on the right track with Glenn.

'What about Stephanie Thornton?'

Harnby sighed. 'You don't give up, do you. What about Ms Thornton?'

'She had no reason to be a fan of Olivia's. Has anything come up on your radar?'

'Sophie, look at me!' She waved a hand the length of her body. 'Do I look like Joe? Do I resemble him in any way? I'm not a walking crime database for you to access whenever you see fit. Look, Stephanie is a respected businesswoman. She's human, like anyone, and has made her mistakes, but that doesn't make her a killer.'

'Talking about those mistakes...'

Harnby threw her head back and laughed. 'You really should join the police. I can see you wearing people out until the confessions come pouring out of them.' She sighed again. 'She didn't try to put up any kind of a fight, either when she was pulled over, or when it came to court. She was as good as gold.'

Harnby was beginning to look a bit annoyed, so I decided to wrap things up.

'She was really unlucky – a taxi company owner with a driving ban, but it sounds like she dealt with it well. Thanks. '

'There was no luck about it. There was an anonymous tip-off. Someone knew she'd been at a dinner and phoned the police when they saw her drive off from the venue. Look, Dad's waiting for me. Am I free to go now?'

I nodded, mulling things over in my head. I was more eager than ever for Saturday night to come around; I wanted to have a chat with Stephanie Thornton. It was time to get to know the woman better.

I stopped Harnby as she turned to join her dad.

'You might not want to head outside, DI Flynn turned up just before you.'

She looked momentarily taken aback, and then collected herself. 'Thanks for the heads up.'

Leaving Harnby to dodge her boss, I set off on the long, gruelling walk home – over the road!

---

17

*I*t was Saturday evening, it was humid, and Joyce and I were heading for Buxton, a famous Derbyshire spa town that was a magnet to visitors from around the world. Its waters had attracted Mary Queen of Scots, and even Erasmus Darwin, grandfather of Charles, had recommended a visit. Just the other side of the town at the top of a long, winding road, partially concealed by trees, was the home of Stephanie Thornton.

'Are we about to spend the evening in the company of a killer? I just want to be prepared.' Joyce sounded utterly serious, and yet not at all concerned.

'There are three people who all seem to have motives. But their reasons for wanting Olivia out of the way would equally be good reasons to stay out of it and avoid the risk of further negative publicity. Olivia has helped put some pretty big spanners into the works of Stephanie's businesses and kept a lot of the issues in the media spotlight, so Stephanie has had to work hard to recover her reputation. I also wonder if Olivia was the one to call the police when Stephanie drove after a few too many drinks. Olivia turned up to protest at a number of dinners – maybe at one of them she'd seen Stephanie drive off in her car. After all, Stephanie had access to plenty of cars and drivers, so seeing her behind the wheel would have immediately been noticeable. Stephanie could still be fuming about that – Glenn made it clear that she has a temper.

'And then there's Amber, who is all about image. She might be behind the scenes, but whatever happens to Stephanie and Glenn has a huge impact on her. Finally, there's your boyfriend.'

'He's not my…'

'I know, I'm kidding. I'm convinced he's not being quite honest with us, though. I'm betting Amber has him well trained for when he talks to the press and he's more than capable of telling only half the story, so I'm hoping he'll relax after a couple of drinks. Maybe you can try to charm more information out of him? See if he has any idea if Stephanie knows whether it was Olivia who told the police she was driving under the influence.'

Joyce chuckled. 'He's been texting me all afternoon, so he's still keen. I'll see what I can do.'

Joyce slowed down as we reached our destination. A forest of rhododendron bushes hid much of the house that lay behind a small metal gate and short driveway. Most of Thorne Cars' staff had been bussed in from the office building in Manchester, but a valet had been hired to take care of the cars of the few who, like us, had driven themselves.

The party was a relaxed affair. An enormous barbecue had its own team of staff and two bars kept everyone lubricated. Lights had been slung between branches of the trees and little tea-lights in jars marked the path to the garden. Jazz music – the kind that crossed over into pop, rather than that which required you to wear a polo neck and dark-rimmed spectacles – could be heard over the chatter. The grey stone house was big enough to be impressive, yet small enough to look like a family home, albeit a very wealthy family.

'Joyce, Sophie, over here.' Glenn was standing by the front

door, chatting to a woman I immediately recognised as Stephanie Thornton. I groaned to myself. Like Joyce, Stephanie was wearing a pair of towering wedge shoes and must have been close to six feet tall. As she loomed over me by the best part of a foot, I felt ridiculous.

Her handshake was firm, but not too firm; her smile seemed genuinely warm and welcoming.

'Glenn told me he had some friends coming,' she said.

'Sorry about that, I hope we haven't messed up your numbers.'

She looked down at me. 'Not at all. Please, come and get a drink.'

We followed her through a beautiful cream and ivory hallway. A table held a vase of the most enormous bouquet of cream roses I had ever seen, and that was despite working somewhere with gardens as grand as those at Charleton House. I glanced up the stairs. Dozens of framed black-and-white photos – family, I assumed – lined the wall.

'We'll go to the kitchen, it's a little quieter in there.'

The kitchen was just as I had expected, all gleaming white surfaces and hidden lighting. The room was essentially in the basement and the patio doors opened out onto a small sunken garden, the noise of the party travelling down.

'I need a break from meeting and greeting; I think I can be permitted fifteen minutes' respite. What can I get you?'

I watched while Stephanie mixed our drinks with the skill of an experienced bartender.

'You have a beautiful home,' I commented, not sure what else to say. It was attractive, although if I was honest, it was far too polished. It belonged in the pages of a home-style magazine and I couldn't get a sense of the owner's personality.

'Thank you, although you're not getting an entirely accurate picture. It's taken two days to get it ready for tonight; normally it looks like a bomb's hit it.'

She handed out the various drinks and I watched as Glenn,

rather unsubtly, steered Joyce out into the garden. He'd probably been hoping to get her alone for days, but I kept turning up.

'It's very generous of you to host your staff.'

'They're less likely to get paralytic at the boss's house, and I can control when they go home. End result, fewer post-hangover recriminations in the office on Monday. So it's less generosity and more my control-freak tendencies coming out.' She finished with a broad smile and a mouthful of her gin and tonic. 'Glenn tells me you run a number of cafés. So you must know what it's like.'

I laughed knowingly. 'I have a fantastic team, but some days I'm not sure whether I'm a manager, a mother, nurse, psychiatrist, relationship coach, or just the devil incarnate. I long ago gave up trying to please everyone.'

'Smart move. That way madness lies.'

There was an openness about Stephanie that I liked. I knew from reading about her that there was toughness to her, which I was convinced I could see in the intense way she focused on me when I spoke, but that made me like her more. I would have to watch my alcohol consumption – a couple more glasses and I'd be revealing my innermost secrets to her.

I watched Glenn and Joyce as they admired the flowerbed that was an explosion of well-manicured colour. Or at least, Joyce pretended to. In reality, she didn't know her peonies from her pansies.

'How did you get involved with Charleton House?' I asked Stephanie idly.

'Through me.'

I hadn't been aware of Amber coming in. She walked straight to the fridge and helped herself to a bottle of beer, removed the cap and stuck a piece of lime in the top.

'I'd worked with the events department there to host a dinner for some foreign cycling dignitaries a couple of years ago.' Amber turned to Stephanie. 'By the way, the bar is getting low on ice, so one of the bar staff is just going to pick some up.'

'How do you run out of ice on a night like this? That's a bit poor.' Stephanie sounded more exasperated than annoyed.

I was surprised by the way Amber treated Stephanie's house like her own home, and couldn't have been doing a good enough job at hiding my confusion. Amber grinned.

'Meet my mum.'

As soon as she said it, I could see it in their faces.

'Aaaah, okay, I had no idea.'

'I don't tend to shout about it, and the different surnames help. I wanted people to take me seriously, not assume that the only reason I was successful was thanks to Mum. Although we do work together.' She took a drink. 'Mum, you should go and mingle, get a few photos with the guests. The photographer's arrived.'

Stephanie nodded. 'Good to meet you, Sophie, enjoy your evening.' She left via the patio, exchanged a few words with Glenn and Joyce, and then disappeared up a small flight of stone stairs.

'Your mum's lucky to have you.'

'It goes both ways. I started my career by helping out with the family business, but yes, I do feel like I've been able to give back.'

She looked out towards Glenn and Joyce.

'Are they serious?'

'Difficult to say, but they seem to be getting on well, and he gives the impression he's keen.' I decided it was best not to mention Joyce's revolving door approach to men.

'He needs a woman on his arm. She's a little older than I was hoping for, and we might have to work on her colour palette, but I'm sure we could make it work.' She sounded a little reluctant about that prospect, and I wondered if she realised just what a hornets' nest she would be sticking her head into by offering fashion advice to the force of nature that was Joyce. I decided to keep my opinions to myself for the time being, though.

Amber jumped off her stool. 'In the meantime, I need to keep an eye on that photographer. Enjoy the party.'

I watched as she stopped to say a few words to Glenn, who looked at his watch and nodded, before she carried on up the stone steps that led into the garden. My guess was she wanted him in some of the photos with Stephanie. Or was it a ploy to get him away from Joyce and her very individual colour palette?

18

'Bugger, I get the impression he really rather likes me,' Joyce said as she handed me another drink and settled down next to me on the picnic blanket I'd found. She didn't seem overjoyed, so maybe Amber's disapproval of her wasn't going to be a problem after all.

'So, what do you think?' she asked as we watched Stephanie pour drinks behind the bar and take a turn at the barbecue. It all seemed a little strange. I wasn't used to parties that didn't include a few corsets or periwigs and weren't attended by a member of the British aristocracy.

'I like her,' I replied.

'I don't care if you like her or not, did she kill Olivia?'

I turned to look at Joyce. 'How the hell would I know?'

'With that combination of women's intuition and your Sherlocking skills.'

'Sherlocking? Really? Well, she has motive enough. But Olivia can't be blamed for the housing project collapsing. She wasn't the judge making the final decision.'

'True, but Olivia is a common denominator in a lot of Stephanie's problems, and after all the hard work she put in,

Stephanie must have been frustrated. And Olivia shopped her to the police.'

I corrected her. 'We still don't know if it was Olivia, and even if it was, whether Stephanie knew about that bit.'

Joyce leant back against a tree and made herself comfortable. She closed her eyes and in a singsong voice replied, 'Yes, we do.' She sounded very pleased with herself. 'This detecting malarkey is really quite easy: flutter your eyelashes, top up their drink...'

'What do you mean, we do? Is that what Glenn told you?' I kicked her foot; I needed her to stop playing it cool and just give me the details.

She opened her eyes and grinned. 'I pretended we already knew, that it was no big deal, and he just confirmed it. Seems Olivia taunted Stephanie with it the other week, trying to make it clear that Stephanie's not as in control of everything as she likes to think.'

'How did Stephanie react? Did he say?'

'Blew her lid initially. Stormed into a meeting he was having with Amber, ranting about it. But then she cooled down and just started planning the company's next steps.' Joyce closed her eyes again. It sounded like Stephanie had moved from an emotional response to a business one, but if she held a grudge and had only recently found out about Olivia's role in her driving ban, then it could have built up until she was mad enough to lash out and strangle her in the heat of the moment.

I was still trying to work out if this put Stephanie further up the list of suspects when Joyce interrupted my thoughts.

'I could get used to this, being taken to parties at nice houses. If Glenn is about to start on a TV career, maybe I should stick around. Who knows where I could be jet-setting off to?'

'You'd have to get past Amber first, make sure you met her standards. There doesn't seem to be much about Glenn's life she doesn't control. Did you know Stephanie's her mum?'

'Really? Well that explains her rocketing up the career ladder before she's out of puberty.'

'She's not that young.'

'She's young enough that she should still be binge drinking with her friends and waking up with vaguely familiar-looking men. She's far too intense for my liking. It's all well and good having a driven mother as a role model, and having "opportunities" thrown at you left, right and centre, but I bet she missed out on a lot.'

Despite Stephanie's best intentions, some of her staff were already getting a little the worse for wear, and a few of the men were taking it in turns to carry each other the length of the garden in a fireman's lift. One pair ran past Glenn and Amber, who were deep in conversation. Amber didn't look particularly happy, and Glenn looked uncomfortable and tense, glancing up from time to time as though checking whether anyone could see him getting a ticking off.

Amber threw her hands in the air and started to walk away. Then she stopped and seemed to give him an order. There was a cold calmness in the way she spoke to him; he didn't look as if he had any choice and followed close on her heels, swigging from a bottle as he went.

'Wait here, I'm just going for a wander.'

Joyce's eyes were still closed. 'Mmmm, fetch me a glass of wine on your way back, will you? A small one.'

I followed the pair back to the house and watched from a distance as Amber led the way through the front door. I could see her storming up the stairs, Glenn on her heels, and wondered how many times this scene had been played out whenever Glenn said or did something that didn't align with her strategic plan, or some such thing.

I was concerned about the level of ambition in this house. It could be that Amber had felt the need to protect all her hard work in relation to Glenn and Thorne Cars, especially as that had turned out to be her family business. Stephanie had many of the same reasons to want Olivia out of the way and I had to remind myself not to be charmed by her.

I reached the top of the stairs in time to see Glenn walk into a room at the far side of the landing. He pushed the door closed behind him, but as it hit the frame, it didn't catch. Instead, it bounced open again. Only by a couple of inches, but enough for me to hear everything Amber was saying.

'...you need to forget her. We're done at that bloody house. You need to stay away and focus on the new contracts; you start filming next month. That should be the only thing on your mind.'

There was a mumble from Glenn that I couldn't make out.

'I don't give a damn how you feel. I already got rid of one for you, I don't want to have to do it again.'

'For me? You didn't do it for me, I didn't ask you to.'

'I know, and I'd like you to start solving your own problems.'

'She wasn't a problem, she was an old friend. What you did was cruel and unnecessary, I won't let you do it again.'

'I don't think you have much say in this. I've revived your career, everything you have is down to me.'

'I get that, and I'm grateful, but my private life is my own.'

'Not anymore, that's not how this works. You're going to be in the public eye, and the public will want to know more than just your opinion on some bike race in the Pyrenees. They'll be especially interested in your love life. Fix this, or I will.'

I'd heard enough and walked in. They both stared at me like rabbits caught in headlights. Amber was the first to compose herself.

'Yes? Are you lost?' she asked coldly. We both knew that my presence was not an accident. 'The party is downstairs.'

'Joyce is not a problem to be fixed. For a start, I'd like to see you try.'

'Sophie, I...' Glenn walked towards me looking tired and sad, but I cut him off.

'You knew what she did? She got rid of your friend, and you said nothing?'

'Sophie, we had just signed the contract. The ink was barely dry. My getting involved wasn't going to help. I figured I could fix it later.'

'Fix what? What are you going to do, bring her back from the dead? I don't understand.'

There was silence as Amber and Glenn stared at me, confusion clear on their faces. Amber laughed out loud as she realised what I meant.

'You think I killed her? Dear God,' she laughed again, 'that's priceless. Stupid bloody woman, I didn't kill anyone. I warned Olivia off, told her a few home truths about her place in the world and to steer clear of Glenn. I'll make sure Jackie gets the message too.'

'Jackie?' Now I was confused.

'Your mate, the one who clearly doesn't own a full-length mirror.'

'Joyce.'

'Whatever,' she said dismissively.

'Amber, that's enough,' Glenn shouted and took a step towards her. It looked like he might have a spine after all.

When they started rowing again, I ignored them. Between them, Glenn and Amber had pretty solid motives. The one other person who slotted into all that was Stephanie, but it really didn't feel right. Stephanie didn't need to kill anyone herself; she'd have had someone else take care of it. It would have been planned, and Olivia's death had always felt spur of the moment. It involved emotion, not a business decision.

I thought about where there had been emotion. Who felt passionately enough about something involving Olivia to snap and kill her?

Glenn and Amber were still arguing when I left the room and ran down the stairs.

19

I found Joyce right where I'd left her.

'You took your time, I'm gasping for a drink.'

'Come on, we're going.' I was out of breath. I pulled Joyce up off the ground and steered her across the lawn towards her car.

'Where? Why? Do I not get a drink?'

'I reckon I know who killed Olivia. You drive, I'll call Harnby.' I got in the car and pulled out my phone.

'Can we put the top down?' Joyce asked.

'I've just told you I know who the killer is and you want us to hold on and put the roof down? No, woman, drive!'

She responded by turning the key in the ignition and setting off so quickly, I nearly knocked myself out on the dashboard. It was going to be the golf cart all over again.

I eventually managed to get Joyce to slow down. There was nothing to be gained by arriving before the police. I knew we wouldn't be welcome at all, but I'd got caught up in the moment.

We parked up the road with the house in sight, but far enough away that we wouldn't be seen by anyone. Then we sat and waited.

'What gave it away?' asked Joyce.

'It was something and nothing. Someone being caught up in the heat of the moment and reacting by killing a woman meant high emotion. Everything has been about cold-hearted business for most people we've spoken to, apart from one.'

We both looked towards the well-kept house in the leafy Macclesfield street. I was thinking about the man who had filled his life with antique bikes after his wife had died, filling the void that she'd left. Howard's interest was in bikes from the surrounding area; for him, it was all about local history, local memories, bikes that had a story that he could relate to. The first bike he'd told me about at Cyclemania had had a family connection.

Howard was clinging on to the past. We all do it to some extent, but he was still grieving, and in all that emotion, he'd taken it a step too far. I remembered the auction site open on Howard's laptop the day I'd last visited his home. I remembered seeing both Olivia and Howard at Cyclemania on their phones a number of times. Had he been trying to get the bike that Olivia had eventually won? After all, he'd wanted the bike badly enough to try to steal it after she'd died.

You'd have to be pretty obsessed to desire something so much, you didn't want to wait until it was sold the normal way and risk losing it again. There had to be a reason for his obsession with that particular bike for his collection. His interest in local bikes meant he would have done his research – the same research Mark had done. If Mark had found out the origins of that bike, then there was no reason that Howard couldn't have got the same information.

'But why that bike?'

'Eh?' It was only when Joyce responded that I realised I'd been speaking out loud.

'The bike that had belonged to Arthur Lumb, and then Florence Ida Adamson. Why was that bike so important to him that he was prepared to stop at nothing in order to get it, not even murder? The bike must have been connected to his obsession,' I continued. 'In other words, his wife.' I turned to look at Joyce. 'What if Mrs Young was descended from Florence Ida Adamson? Or Arthur Lumb?'

'So *that's* why you asked Harnby if she knew what his wife's maiden name was when you called her on the way here.'

My mind drifted back one week, to the memory of the live interpreter I'd seen at Charleton House on the day of Cyclemania, dressed as Arthur Lumb. I remembered the feeling of having seen the young soldier's ghost, so convincing had the portrayal been.

'If we're right and she was related to Arthur Lumb, I wonder, because of his grief, if the combination of seeing his wife's ancestor apparently risen from the dead on Saturday and losing out on getting the bike that Arthur had once ridden pushed Howard far enough to kill Olivia. I was stupid to get side-tracked by the idea of a respectable retired head teacher not being the criminal kind.'

'And he just took the opportunity at Cyclemania?' Joyce asked.

'Betsy said that Olivia had seemed really happy. If she knew she'd secured the bike, that meant Howard knew he'd lost it. That evening, it would have been easy enough for him to tell her he wanted to talk and lead her somewhere more private, away from everyone else into the shadows of the garden. The film has a pretty constant soundtrack that would have been loud enough to cover the sound of any arguing, neither of them had attended the event with anyone else, so no one would have noticed them missing, and it turned out that Howard had the perfect murder weapon in his goody bag. It might even have been in his pocket, if he'd taken it out to look at it.'

'What did Harnby say when you asked about Howard's wife?'

'Not much. Just a long pause, and then "I'll check". I reckon I'll get stern words when she next sees me.'

'Well get ready, then.'

Two police cars had arrived, closely followed by an unmarked car. I watched as Harnby got out. She was about to cross the road when she looked in our direction; she'd seen Joyce's rather distinctive car before when we were at Olivia's. She stood and stared at us for a couple of seconds, and then walked to the house.

'Should we go?' asked Joyce.

'No, she's seen us. We may as well wait and get our wrists slapped now, get it over and done with. There's also the distinct possibility that I'm wrong about all of this.'

What felt like hours later, but it was probably only thirty minutes, we saw Howard being led out to a car by two uniformed officers. Even from a distance up the road, he looked like a tired old man. For a moment, I felt painfully sorry for him.

'I hope Harnby says thank you,' said Joyce, turning away from the house to face me.

I'd seen all I needed to see. 'Let's go,' I said. 'If she turns up at the pub again, she can buy me a drink.'

Joyce made no move to start the car. 'I forgot to tell you, when I came to pick you up and drove past the pub, Harnby and Flynn were talking in the car park. Another man was with them,' she said conspiratorially.

'That was probably Harnby's father.' My heart sank at the thought of Detective Inspector Flynn in my local, again. 'I don't mind Harnby, but Flynn I'm not so keen on. We'll have to tell him there's been talk of food poisoning at the Black Swan, or the beer's off.'

Joyce's face fell as she looked over my shoulder.

'Food poisoning? When?'

I hadn't noticed Harnby walk up to join us. Joyce smiled awkwardly.

'How much of that did you hear?' I asked.

'Enough to know that you don't mind me, which I think I'm flattered by.' She leaned over and propped herself up on the edge of my window.

'It's nothing personal, not really. It's just, we've seen you and Flynn in the Black Swan a few times recently, and… well, I can't imagine Joe finding that particularly relaxing. I'm surprised to see you hanging out with Flynn, anyway; he doesn't exactly come across as much fun.'

'He's not. Never has been, not even when I was a kid.'

That took the wind out of my sails. 'A kid… you were… he was… what?'

She laughed. 'That stumped you. Look, don't tell anyone, not even Joe, promise? Promise?'

'I don't know what I'm not telling him, but I promise.'

Beside me, Joyce nodded her agreement.

'DI Flynn is my uncle. Dad is staying with me while Mum's away at a yoga retreat with friends, and he wants to spend time with his brother. DI Flynn and I agreed not to let on that we're related when I transferred from Manchester. It's still tough being a woman in my job and the last thing I need is people thinking the only reason I got promoted, or get promoted further in the future, is because of nepotism.'

I exchanged glances with Joyce.

'You have our word,' I said. 'But why choose the Swan? It's a bit close to home.'

'Any pub round here was a risk, and Dad had done a lot of research on the best pubs for craft beer. He kept wanting to return and I didn't want to disappoint him, so I took my chances. You won't see us there again.'

'Okay, thanks. Well, for the Flynn bit. I'm sure you're good company.'

She laughed. 'You can put the shovel down now. I doubt Joe would want me turning up in his local.'

I looked down the road towards Howard's house. 'You got your man?'

'We did.' She pulled a small plastic bag out of her pocket. Inside was a flattened cardboard box. I peered at it; it had previously held an inner tube. 'I guess the old boy was used to his wife emptying his pockets for him.'

'Is that going to be enough?' I wondered.

'Right now, all he's saying is "I'm sorry". I don't think it will be long until a confession comes pouring out of him.' I nodded, and Harnby spoke again. 'We got this thanks to a particularly helpful tip-off, for which I'm very grateful.' She smiled. 'I might have a few questions for you later. Maybe you could both head to the Black Swan and I'll see you there... I'm kidding.'

I laughed and shook my head. Flynn might not have much of a sense of humour, but his niece certainly did.

*a*fter a lie in, which came to an abrupt end when Pumpkin decided it was time for me to get up and lay on my chest staring unblinkingly at me, and following two espressos and a couple of rounds of raisin and cinnamon toast, I was ready to get baking. Joyce and I had ended our Saturday night adventures in the Black Swan after all, where we'd found Mark and Bill enjoying a 'date night'. Following my third gin and tonic, and once we'd filled our friends in on the case conclusion, I'd decided it would be a great idea to invite everyone round for a picnic lunch in my garden the following day. I was determined to serve up a decent scone and this was my last chance.

I stared at the oven and wondered if I really needed to bother. Then I thought about strawberry jam and clotted cream. I wanted... no, I *needed* scones today. Pumpkin was sitting, sphinx-like, on the kitchen table. I was pretty sure she wouldn't turn down clotted cream either.

I covered the garden table with a red gingham cloth, used a small bunch of lavender in a milk bottle as decoration, and placed a full ice bucket in the middle of the table. Joyce worked on the basis of 'It's five o'clock somewhere, or it has been, or it will be', so I added a bottle of English sparkling wine to the ice. The weather forecast had warned that the steaming hot weather might be coming to an end a little earlier than we would have liked and I wanted to play on the English summer theme a little longer. English sparkling wine is also a lot better than many people realise; one producer is a favourite of the Queen, who has probably consumed enough fizz in her lifetime of receptions and dinners to have plenty to pick her favourite from.

'Coo-eeee, it's only us.' I heard the thud, thud, thud of Mark's crutches down the hallway. 'With your track record of putting away murderers, I'm not sure you should be leaving your front door unlocked.'

'I only did that because I knew you were all coming.' I gave him a hug and pulled out a chair for him. After I'd rested his crutches against the wall of the house, I gave Bill a kiss. He raised a bag in the air.

'Home-made quiche, hummus, and an array of crudités. I'll go and prepare them.' As he went into the kitchen to plate up the food, Mark patted the seat next to him.

'So, tell me she's a useless Watson. Always getting distracted by men, has no historical knowledge that could be useful, aaaaand... uses her beauty to seduce the villain and get a confession out of them.'

Joyce smacked the back of Mark's head. I'd seen her do it before and it never failed to make me laugh. It also resulted in the purest 'thwack' sound I'd ever heard.

'You need to work on your timing, Mark Boxer.'

'Do that again, will you, Joyce?' Bill placed the quiche on the table and leant in for a kiss. 'How I've resisted breaking his other leg, I've no idea. Do any of you fancy taking over the role of Florence Nightingale?'

Joyce and I looked at each other. 'I'll put these on a plate.' She took her box of food to the kitchen.

'And I'll get glasses,' I added quickly.

'Rotten sods, the lot of you,' said Mark as he reached for the bottle. 'I'll do the important work, as usual.'

The quiche was creamy and packed full of ham and cheese. The crust was thin and crispy, and I briefly considered offering Bill a job in the kitchens at Charleton House. Joyce was telling the two men about the party the night before – again – but to be honest, I was a little tired of thinking about it all. Wondering about whether or not someone had reason to end another person's life was both exhausting and depressing.

Bill appeared to pick up on my reticence to go over the whole thing again, so after allowing Joyce and Mark to cluck over how I'd reached my murderous conclusion for a few minutes, he kindly changed the subject.

'Joyce, are you and Glenn going to keep in touch, or does the search for Mr Right go on?'

'I'm having far too much fun to call the search off. Glenn is a sweet man, but he follows the instructions of the women in his life far too easily for my liking.' That took us all by surprise. 'I like someone who'll stand up to me. Life is far more interesting with a bit of to and fro.'

I gathered the plates, and as I filled the dishwasher, I heard Mark make his ungainly way into the house. He pushed the door closed behind him.

'Sophie, I wanted a quick word. There's something I thought you might want to know.'

I pointed at a kitchen chair.

'I'm fine. I was thinking about Howard and the Lumb family connection. I'm afraid that all of Howard's murderous efforts may have been for naught.'

'Go on.'

'Arthur Lumb was raised in London. He came to Derbyshire after the war because he had family here.'

'You already told me that.'

'I spent half the night online, trying to iron out a niggle I had about all this. I'm on a lot of those genealogy sites – they're really useful for my research, plus you can access a crazy amount of information now. I traced the Lumb family line forward to see where Howard's wife fitted into the picture, and she doesn't.'

'She doesn't? She's not a Lumb?'

'She's a Lumb alright, but not a Derbyshire Lumb. Her family are from Yorkshire, and I can't find any connection between them and Arthur. There may well be one, but far enough back for it not to be of any real significance. If Howard did believe there was a connection between Arthur Lumb's bike and his wife, it was purely assumption on his part that because they shared such an unusual surname, they must be closely related.'

That silenced me. I briefly wondered if there was any way that information could be kept from Howard, but I guessed it would come out in the trial.

'Are you alright?' Mark put his hand gently on my shoulder.

'Mmmm, yeah. It's just rather sad.'

'I can shine a positive light on all this in another way.'

'Please.'

'Over the last week, I've been able to find records of some of the work that Arthur Lumb carried out in his role of carpenter at Charleton, and he was pretty talented. A lot of his work is still in situ. I had a quiet word with the Duke and he has agreed that we can put together a small exhibition about Arthur with some examples of work. It'll go in one of the empty stables that we use for temporary exhibitions, talking about his life, the bicycle regiment and all the work he did here. We'll also produce a handout that shows where to see the more interesting examples of his work in the house. I've worked out an agreement with the Buxton Museum and we'll get the bike for a couple of months before they put it on display. It's a bit of silver lining that a lot more people are going to hear about Arthur and his life.'

I kissed Mark on the cheek.

'You're a good man, Mark Boxer.'

'I know that!' he exclaimed. 'Can you just make sure that bloody woman knows too?' I laughed. Joyce loved him as much as I did, and he was well aware of that.

Pumpkin had settled on Joyce's knee by the time Mark and I went back outside.

'You look like a James Bond villain,' he commented. 'Careful, she's riddled with fleas and will take a chunk out of your hand if you look at her wrong.'

'Mark, you know none of that's true,' I cried out. 'Your moment of compassion was short-lived.'

'Kitty cat knows I'm only joking,' he said in a horrible baby voice and reached out to stroke her. Pumpkin peered in his direction through half-closed eyes, daring him to get any closer.

'Yeah, maybe not.' He withdrew his hand and sneered at her.

I handed around the plate of scones to some favourable sounds of approval. I'd warmed them slightly in the oven. Splitting one open, I spread a nice, thick dollop of jam, then piled on a mountain of clotted cream.

Mark took the spoon from me and added some to his scone.

'WHAT ARE YOU DOING?' shouted Joyce. 'Do you know nothing?'

Mark looked at his scone with an expression of utter confusion as Joyce continued.

'Jam before cream, every time. Those Devon lot haven't got a clue what they're doing.'

Mark looked at me, clearly lost for words, and lost in general. I licked cream off my fingers, and then explained.

'People in Devon add the cream first, followed by the jam, but they're just crazy. The Cornish have it right: jam first, and then cream. Wars have been fought over less.'

'What have wars been fought over? Your door was unlocked, so I just let myself in.' Detective Constable Joe Greene grinned. 'Got room for a small one?'

We all shuffled round, hugs, kisses and handshakes were exchanged, and another glass filled. Then Joe looked at Mark.

'How come I return from a motorcycle trip unscathed, and yet you're up to your eyeballs in plaster?'

'Mark decided to train for the Tour de France. Needless to say, his entry has been delayed,' Bill replied. Joe laughed, while Mark scowled at his husband.

'Any other less obvious news, Sophie? You got yourself mixed up in anything untoward?'

I looked at the others, and then shook my head. 'Nah, life has been pretty quiet round here.' I'd leave Harnby to fill him in when he got back to work. He was still technically on holiday and I wanted him to maintain his buzz for as long as possible.

'That's not entirely true,' Joyce was giving me an intense stare, 'is it, Sophie?'

'Joyce, let him…'

'These scones, they're delicious, but next time you should do a better job of hiding the packaging. Someone popped out to the local bakery this morning and is passing their famous scones off as her own. Check her rubbish bin for clues, officer, you'll find the bag in there, just under the coffee grounds. She has a pretty solid case of deception to answer for.'

If you enjoyed *A Deadly Ride* then you'll love **Mulled Wine and Murder**. It's Christmas at Charleton House and Sophie has two mysteries to solve. It seems that someone is failing to embrace the goodwill of the season.

The fabulous and formidable Joyce Brocklehurst has her own series of books. Be sure to join her and friend Ginger Salt as they investigate a royal murder in *Murder En Suite.*

READ THE NEXT CHARLETON HOUSE MYSTERY

If you enjoyed A Deadly Ride you'll love

Mulled Wine and Murder.

The glow of a million fairy lights and the hauntingly familiar melodies of Christmas carols fill the vast halls of Charleton House, but when a group of volunteers fall ill after drinking mulled wine laced with poisonous berries, Catering Manager and part-time sleuth Sophie Lockwood wonders who's failing to embrace the goodwill of the season.

'Perfect holiday mystery read.'
'Wonderful characters, historical insights, mystery and excitement, and writing which never disappoints.'
'A fun read for the holidays … Adams doesn't disappoint.'
'The Charleton House Mystery series just gets better and better.'
'Reading each book is like coming home after a long day and enjoying time with friends.'

READ A FREE CHARLETON HOUSE MYSTERY

Building a relationship with my readers is one of the best things about writing. I occasionally send newsletters with details on new releases, special offers, interviews and articles relating to The Charleton House Mysteries.

Sign up to my mailing list and you'll also receive the very first Charleton House Mystery, *A Stately Murder*.

Head to my website for your free copy and find out what happens when Sophie stumbles across the victim of the first murder Charleton House has ever known.

www.katepadams.com

ABOUT THE AUTHOR

After 25 years working in some of England's finest buildings, Kate P. Adams has turned to murder.

Kate grew up in Derbyshire, the setting for the Charleton House Mysteries, and went on to work in theatres around the country, the Natural History Museum - London, the University of Oxford and Hampton Court Palace. Every day she explored darkened corridors and rooms full of history behind doors the public never get to enter. Kate spent years in these beautiful buildings listening to fantastic tales, wondering where the bodies were hidden, and hoping that she'd run into a ghost or two.

Kate has an unhealthy obsession with finding the perfect cup of coffee, enjoys a gin and tonic, and is managed by Pumpkin, a domineering tabby cat who is a little on the large side. Now that she lives in the USA, writing the Charleton House Mysteries allows Kate to go home to be her beloved Derbyshire everyday, in her head at least.

ACKNOWLEDGEMENTS

Thank you to my wonderful beta readers Joanna Hancox, Lynne McCormack, Helen McNally, Eileen Minchin, and Rosanna Summers. Your honesty and insightful comments help make my books so much better than they would otherwise be.

Many thanks to my advance readers, your support and feedback means a great deal to me. Thank you to all my readers.

Thank you to David Hingley for reminiscing about the 2012 Olympics, to Scotford Lawrence from the National Cycle Museum in Wales, and David Stout for his horticultural guidance.

Richard Mason, my police advisor who guides me on procedure and makes sure I am, largely, within the law. When I break the rules, that's all me!

My fabulous editor, Alison Jack, and Julia Gibbs, my eagle-eyed proofreader. Both are a joy to work with.

Fellow author Laura Durham has given me great support and guidance.

Thank you to Susan Stark, who remains calm despite the amount of time her wife spends researching methods of murder.

Printed in Great Britain
by Amazon